BIRDIE

BIRDIE

A GOLF STORY

Tony Rosa

Jackpot PRESS

Birdie

Copyright © 2012 by Anthony J. Rosa

Purchase through booksellers or by contacting:
Jackpot Press
P.O. Box 594
Ft. Lauderdale, FL 33302-0594
or
JackpotPress@gmail.com

This is a work of fiction. All of the characters, names, incidents, places,
organizations, and dialogue in this novel are either the products
of the author's imagination or are used fictitiously.

ISBN: 978-0-9828225-5-5

Library of Congress Control Number: 2011962701

BIRDIE

WEEK ONE

Mark Crowe ducked under a hackberry tree to wait out the storm. He flinched with each clap of thunder and tried to hide from the fuming clouds as they hovered near. Rattling leafage and staggering branches made for a poor shelter. He never had much of chance. His whole life felt that way; stranded in the middle of nowhere with chaos swirling around him. A familiar lonesome feeling came upon him. He couldn't pinpoint what it meant. Most of the time, he didn't even care. Leaning against the water-stained trunk, Mark had no way to know, but in twenty-five weeks, he would find that something and his outlook would be different.

Mark touched at his wet cheek. *I can't believe that little punk took a swing at me.* With his recent history, he couldn't afford even a hint of trouble.

When it didn't clear, he grabbed the heavy bag by the handle and trudged on through the squall. Five minutes later, he waded around a puddle blocking the broken gate, kicked through the knee-high weeds, and lit upon the back porch. Chilled and shaken as if he'd abandoned ship, he pushed open the door. "It's me."

Inside was dim. The overflowing trashcan he had promised to empty greeted him. He tugged at the window shade to let in some light. The greasy smell of pork chops lingered in the air. A skillet soaked in the sink. The refrigerator hummed.

Granny waddled into the kitchen. "Let me get you something." She disappeared into the pantry.

Mark dropped the bag on the floor. He had lugged the deadweight for what felt like miles. He suddenly felt like a lifeguard having just pulled a body from the surf. "I wasn't sure I was going to make it."

"Wait, wait," Granny said. "Wipe off first."

Too late; rainwater puddled on the floor. Mark teetered on the worn linoleum, drenched and exhausted.

"It was so nice earlier." Granny shook her head and glanced out the window. She draped a worn towel over his waiting hand.

"You were in bed when I came home for lunch," he said, shrouding his face.

"Why didn't you knock?"

"I thought maybe you were sleeping."

Mark rolled the soaked tank top over his head and wrapped the towel around his neck. He pulled a chair from the kitchen table and plunged into it. He unlaced his boots. It was no surprise to see his socks drip.

Granny sat and took a sip from a steaming cup. "How'd you do?"

"Considering it was my first time in a long while, not too bad."

"And how were Pappy's clubs?"

"Better than anyone else's."

"Pappy would be proud." Granny glanced at the ceiling where paint chips flaked and dusty cobwebs loitered.

Mark smiled. "I thought about him while I was out there." He remembered Pappy and how often he had returned from the same golf course and sat at the same kitchen table. "But you know—" Mark put on a serious face. "I did get a few dirty looks."

"I told you to be ready for that. I'm sure there's a lot of folks over there still pretty sore at you." She leaned over and patted his hand.

"I got some good news." Mark decided to shift gears. "I made a birdie."

"Oh, that's wonderful." Granny's face lit up. "Pappy would be so proud."

"You should've seen it," he said, trying to sound like Pappy. "I smacked it right down the fairway, whacked it right on the green, and then knocked it right in the hole." Only difference, when Pappy reported making a birdie, you could bet your life he actually accomplished such a feat.

"Well I'll be." Granny smiled. "Pappy played many rounds with those clubs. He pulled them around that old course almost everyday for twenty years. If they could talk, they'd probably tell you where to go on each hole."

Sometimes Granny is still kinda funny. Mark smiled and mopped his long hair with the towel.

Granny pushed herself up from the table and started work on dinner. As she reached high in a cabinet for applesauce, she let out a moan. She pierced the lid with a can opener. Turning the crank appeared to exhaust her. She clutched the bottom of her worn apron to dry her knobby fingers.

With his head buried in the towel, Mark said, "Did my mom call?"

"No dear," Granny turned away from the countertop. "Not today." She entered the cupboard and emerged with a bag of rolls. "I did hear from your sister. She said she wanted to bring the boys by for a visit soon."

Mark remained perched in his seat with the towel draped over his head. Every few minutes he took a peek. Granny stirred pots on the stovetop and kept watch on a pan baking in the oven. Mark heard a knock. "Granny, I think someone's at the front door."

Granny flipped a switch that cutoff the exhaust fan. "What's that dear?"

"I said I think someone's at the front door." *Silly old duck needs a hearing aid.*

"Let's see who that could be."

Granny shuffled towards the entrance in her cloth slippers. Mark followed, poking a dry chunk of the towel into an ear. Granny drew back the faded drape and glanced through the side glass.

"It's the police," she said, looking confused.

Panic swept through Mark. "I have to tell you something." He straight-armed the door and blocked her from opening it.

"What is it dear?"

"I was only trying to be nice to these guys." Mark spat out the words as if rehearsing them. "And this kid hauls off and hits me. I was just showing these guys a trick. I was trying to be friendly. And this one kid started a fight."

"Oh my." Granny shook her head and stared at the floor. "You know you're supposed to be staying out of trouble."

"Oh definitely. I know Granny, and I tried. You have to believe me. If they ask about it, you have to tell them I did nothing wrong. It wasn't my fault. I was trying to be their friend."

"You're supposed to just walk away from any trouble."

"I know. But you have to believe me on this one. I didn't start anything. Believe me Granny." Mark grabbed her hand. "No matter what they say, that boy hit me first. Don't let them tell you any different—no matter what."

Mark moved aside and she opened the door.

"Evenin' ma'am," an officer said, tipping his cap. "I'm Officer Bellamy—this is my partner, Officer Gagnon. Is there a Mark Crowe that lives here?"

Fear made Mark's stomach twist into a tight knot. Any hopes that they were at the wrong house vanished. He remained behind the door and stole a look through the side window. The one doing the talking held a small spiral notepad and wore a clear plastic poncho over his uniform. What looked like a shower cap covered his brimmed hat.

"That's my grandson," Granny said, gripping the doorknob like a walking cane. "He's drying off."

"We'd like to talk with him," the officer continued with a patient voice.

Granny's free hand shook more than normal. "Can I ask what this is all about?"

Mark saw the other cop. It appeared the conditions were not extreme enough to intimidate him into raingear. He glared at Granny while both thumbs were tucked into his shiny gun belt.

"Well, ma'am." The cop looked at his notepad. "The reason we're here is there was a complaint over at the golf course about some kids throwing golf balls at cars."

When Granny glanced behind the door, Mark shook his head. Wet ends of his hair swept across the towel.

Granny shook her head in unison. She turned back to the inquisitors. "That couldn't be my Mark."

"This happened today, not long ago, ma'am. We've been tracking down who might be involved. Luke Dengel over at the golf course said we should talk to Mark."

"Well, like I said, it couldn't be my Mark."

Stupid old Dingleberry. Just the mention of Luke Dengel made Mark uneasy. *Why'd he go and point the cops at my house? Always on my case. I don't care if he was friends with Pappy.*

"Just the same, ma'am, we'd like to speak to him."

"Wait just a minute." Granny closed the door.

Mark whispered, "It wasn't me Granny."

"I believe you sweetheart," she said. "But please don't get smart with them. You know you can't afford any more trouble."

"Oh, for sure. I know."

"Stay calm now." She turned the doorknob while Mark stood behind her. "This is my grandson, Mark."

The cop with his paws gripping the holster finally spoke. "You know anything about throwing golf balls at cars?"

"No, man—" Mark shook his head. "I don't know what you're talking about."

"The person that complained described someone that looked just like you."

"Well, it wasn't me." Mark did his best to stay calm.

"We radioed in your name and got your address—" the same cop said, turning his head towards the adjacent wall. He ran his index finger across the siding, looked at it and smirked. "We know you've been in trouble before."

The cop holding the notepad looked at Granny and smiled. "This wouldn't be Colonel Crowe's house would it?"

"It is," she said.

"I play with the *Orphans* over at the golf course. I remember the Colonel—even played with him a few times."

"How nice." Granny smiled. "He was with that group near twenty years."

"I know a lot of people miss him. How long's he been gone now?"

"Coming up on eight years."

"Wow, doesn't seem that long."

"Mark is his grandson," Granny said.

Mark hoped the endorsement might help.

It didn't appear to impress the cop next to the wall. "We know you're on probation—in the aftercare program," he said. "Who's your case manager?"

Mark looked at the ground. "His name is Mr. Shannon. I meet with him in the administration building."

"You know we'll be telling him about this."

"C'mon man." Mark snapped his head back up. "Tell him about what? I said I didn't know what you were talking about."

The cop pulled the pointer finger out again and waved it at Mark. "We know it was you."

"Oh my," Granny placed her hand over her mouth.

"You know, we could run you in." He glanced over at his partner. "We should run him in."

"C'mon, man." Mark continued to shake his head. "It wasn't me."

The cop with the notepad finally spoke. "Since no one can actually identify you as the perpetrator, there's not much we can do. And if you say it wasn't you, then—"

Mark exhaled.

"But know one thing," the other cop said. "We'll be watching you."

"Ma'am." The cordial cop tipped his hat again.

The other cop's stare seemed to penetrate the closing door like a laser beam.

"Oh, sweetheart—" Granny leant back on the closed door. "You've got to stay out of trouble."

"It wasn't me Granny," Mark said, leading the way back to the kitchen.

"But if you're even around or near any trouble they'll come and get you."

"I know that." Mark grabbed the church calendar hanging from a bare nail. He sat at the table and leafed through it. "I know what I'm supposed to do. I got to make it to my eighteenth birthday. Once I reach eighteen, the judge said they would sponge my record."

Granny looked confused. "Sponge your record?"

"Yeah," Mark nodded. "You know, sponge it clean." He counted down the rows of weeks. "Seven, eight, nine—" Each month came with a different saint. "My probation is over. Sixteen, seventeen, eighteen—" He flipped past a portrait of the Good Samaritan and counted the last few rows. "I'll be a legal adult in twenty-five weeks. No more probation. No more hassles. No more trouble. Anybody can stay out of trouble for twenty-five weeks."

Definitely.

WEEK TWO

Mark grew tired of waiting in the cramped office. The buzzing fluorescent tubes irritated him and the worn carpet emitted a musty smell. After glancing at the clock more times than he could remember, he stood and read the framed certificates on the wall. When his case manager finally appeared alongside the doorjamb, Mark turned to him and said, "What's a *piss college?*"

"That's psychology," said Mr. Shannon, the case manager. He pointed at the threadbare chair at the front of his desk. "Have a seat."

"I thought you went to some school where they taught you to go around taking a leak on everything."

"Very funny." The case manager scratched his scalp and grinned. A dated tie hung in a loose knot around his permanent-press collar, and an I.D. badge flapped on his breast pocket. "Some people might even say that's exactly what I do."

Mark wiggled into the seat cushion. He leaned a forearm on the cluttered desktop and drummed his fingers. "You ever get tired of this place?"

"Sometimes."

"If I had to deal with juvenile delinquents all day, I think I'd end up taking one of those big books off your shelf and smashing my head with it."

"Thanks for being honest."

Mark started to say, "You're welcome," but instead he went with, "I'm always honest."

"Always, huh?" The case manager raised an eyebrow. "Do I detect a little sarcasm?"

"You sure like throwing around those fancy words."

"Sarcasm? That's not that fancy. But I thought we got past all the hostile feelings in our first session."

"You call this hostile?"

"No. I just want you to be open and comfortable. Like I explained last time, I'm not here to punish you or even judge you. I'm here to help."

"Whatever." *This guy is so full of it his eyes are brown.*

"I hope there won't be a need to explain that every time we get together." The case manager entwined his fingers, placed them behind his head, and tilted back in the chair. "Now, let me use a tired cliché. What's on your mind? What should we talk about?"

"I guess last time wasn't so bad—after I thought about it and all." Mark looked at the ceiling. "I've come to the conclusion that bad luck just seems to follow me around."

"That's interesting." The case manager leaned forward. "You want to explain?"

"Remember how you thought it would be a good idea for me to play in that golf tournament?"

"If you recall, we both agreed to it. We both agreed that it was a good way to get you back into the 'swing of things'. Pardon the pun." The case manager loved relaying ideas with clichés and often drew quotation marks in the air as he fired them. "We both thought you shouldn't avoid things that create problems for you. Wasn't it your first time playing golf in more than a year?"

Mark swept his long hair from his face with a nod. "Almost two years." He patted at the pocket of his sleeveless flannel shirt and dug out a crumpled pack of cigarettes. "They stuck me in the last group—said it was to keep an eye on me."

"If you remember, that was part of what we agreed." The case manager frowned. "I hope you're not planning to smoke."

"Why not?"

"Like I told you last time, it's a dumb and dangerous habit that could eventually kill you."

"Oh yeah." Mark stuffed the cigarette back into the pack. *One more hassle.*

"Beyond a lack of respect for my wishes, it also doesn't display much intelligence, you know, to break the law in front of your probation officer." The chair squeaked as he rocked. "Does your grandmother let you smoke?"

"She doesn't say anything about it." *Then again, she usually doesn't catch me.*

"Does she have any rules?"

"Oh yeah." Mark had become accustomed to answering such questions. In order to sound convincing, he learned to emphasize and exaggerate his answers. "She's very strict."

"I'd bet you have a lot of freedom."

"You'd lose that bet." Mark often let his imagination take over. *The more outlandish, the more likely they'll believe me.* He stared at a water-stained tile in the ceiling. "She even has the rules posted."

"Grandparents are known to be less stringent."

"Not Granny. And, since you brought up the subject, you know that question you asked about last time, about who would be my perfect dad?"

"I recall the discussion being something like that."

"I've been thinking a lot about that," Mark said. "You know who I wish I had for a Dad?"

"Who?"

"Willie Nelson."

"Willie Nelson?"

"Oh, definitely. Yeah, the red-headed stranger. He'd make a great dad."

"How so?"

"He'd never hassle me about getting a haircut. He'd tell me stories about being on the road. He wouldn't care about the smoking, and he'd never hassle me about what I'm wearing. I'd even get to listen to him practice on that guitar of his. I wouldn't even need a radio. I'd be the son of a real outlaw. Or was it a highwayman?"

"So you think Willie Nelson would be perfect?"

"He wouldn't be bad." Mark learned from experience that a little anger got your point across. It also showed you were being sincere. He drew his eyebrows closer and used a lower voice. "This wasn't easy for me to come up with you know."

"I realize that, and I thank you for thinking about it."

"Back in boot camp, I would've gotten some real points for that answer."

"You feel like that is important?"

"What?"

"Earning points."

"That's how it works ain't it?"

"Not really."

Mark had breezed through his incarceration. He shared housekeeping duties and the food wasn't bad. Although the day's schedule within the minimally-secured facility was regimented, he imagined far worse scenarios. Counselors emphasized rehabilitation as their goal, but covert conversations between detainees always included illicit plans to continue down the same crooked path.

"C'mon man," Mark said, "if that's not how it works, then why'd they have me sitting in a circle with a bunch of losers for three months, listening to their loser stories. They cried like babies over the stupidest things. You know, none of them even knew how to do laundry?"

"That's interesting."

"Biggest crybabies I ever saw." Mark shook his head. "Most of 'em didn't know how to even fix their own dinner. When it came time to eat or wash clothes, they all looked to me. I've been doing that stuff my whole life. I figured everybody knew how to, but they didn't. And boy did they whine about it."

"That's interesting."

"I'd hear even more complaining when we sat around in that circle—about the simplest stuff. A terrible childhood. Mommy or Daddy smacking 'em around. Or, how somebody else had abused them."

"Had you ever heard of such things before?"

"I've heard things. And, look, I know a lowlife when I see one. This one kid in our neighborhood, he used to pull wings off of flies and stuff like that. He had this magnifying glass he liked to use on worms. He like, got off on watching these worms wiggling while they fried. Now that's a messed-up dude for you."

"And where is he today?"

"I don't know."

"Back to your time at Rayburn—did you gain anything from the experience?"

Mark dropped his head allowing his long hair to hide his face. He knew to be careful with the answer. "I'm not sure."

"When it was your turn, did you 'share' your thoughts?"

Again with the fingers in the air.

"Sure." That was a lie.

"What did you talk about?"

"I came up with my own stories about my terrible childhood."

Satisfied that he had performed well, Mark leaned back and balanced his weight on the two back legs of the chair. He tried to look exhausted from divulging so much.

"I got a call from an Officer Bellamy," the case manager said. "He told me about a complaint over at the golf course."

The front two legs of Mark's chair slammed to the floor. Mark sat quietly, trying not to overreact. "Like I said, bad luck seems to follow me around."

"He said some kids were throwing golf balls at cars."

"Yeah man, I played in the tournament that day, just like we agreed." Mark nodded his head and hurried his words. "And yeah, I didn't even tell the cops about this one kid that hauled off and threw a punch at me. All I was trying to do was make friends. And what did I get for it? A punch in the face and the cops knocking on my door."

"And you feel that all your troubles followed you to the golf course?"

"Hey man—" Mark felt his cool slipping. "They came to my house hassling me. They got Granny all worked up over nothing."

"They had every right to question you, but from what I understand, they didn't have any solid proof you were involved."

"That's exactly what I said." Mark leaned back in the chair again and locked his fingers behind his head. "Besides, I've put myself on this timeline. I've got a plan now. I've looked on the calendar and everything. You see, I won't be doing nothing wrong until I'm eighteen. Once I hit eighteen, all my problems will go away."

The case manager remained quiet while looking out the door. "Anyway—" He looked back at Mark. "We've been trying to think about your community service and it was Officer Bellamy that gave me the idea."

"I thought we agreed on highway litter patrol."

"We talked about it, but I haven't officially committed. I think what Officer Bellamy suggested may be better. Before you got here today, I made a call. It's an organization that might be a good fit for you. Better yet, it's close enough that you could walk."

"Walk?"

"Yes, if everyone agrees, you can do your community service at the golf course."

Mark thought about his bad luck there. His first reaction was to disagree. Instead, he remembered the timeline. *You can make it to your eighteenth birthday. Just be cool.* "Work at the golf course?"

"Something like that."

Raking sand bunkers or picking up range balls...not bad. Way easier than highway litter patrol. Even if I have to empty a few garbage cans. Mark grinned. "Hey, you know who likes to play golf?"

"Who?"

"Willie Nelson."

Week Three

Mark stepped over the threshold and glanced around the clubhouse. Racks of labeled hats and shirts tempted the curious golfers standing in line to pay their greens fee. Across the room, a man, matching the description of the person he was scheduled to meet, sat at one of the round concession stand tables. He was like a statue. The fingertips of one hand touched the rim of a Styrofoam cup while the other hand rested flat atop the table next to a collapsed cane. Circling his round doughy face was the brim of a bucket hat. Combined with the dark glasses, he looked like Roy Orbison on a fishing trip.

Mark approached, head lowered, his long hair covering his face. "Ah-hum—" He cleared his voice. "I think you're the person I'm supposed to meet with."

"Hi ya, kid." The man smiled, but didn't turn his head. "I'm Victor Adano." He stuck out a hand vaguely aimed in Mark's direction. "Most people just call me Vic."

"My name's Mark." He took the hand and shook. "Mark Crowe." The fingertips felt sweltering.

"Have a seat."

Mark sat across the table and scanned the room. It was the first time he had ever spoken to someone like Vic.

"My wife dropped me off early, so I thought I'd get a cup of coffee before we head out. You want anything?"

"Nah." Mark noticed a woman sitting by herself two tables over. She appeared suspiciously interested in his arrival. Her occasional glances only heightened the feeling.

"So you're a big golfer, eh?"

"Not really." Mark shrugged. "As a matter of fact, I seem to have bad luck around this golf course."

"You worried about any of it rubbing off on me?"

"I guess that's for you to worry about." *Wonder how he goes to the toilet?*

"Not me, kid. I try not to worry about much of anything." Vic shook his head. "Here's a little tip for you—I'm not hard of hearing.

Know what I mean? You don't have to talk any louder or slower. Just talk normal."

Maybe it was a little loud. Mark decided to push forward. "You got one of them seeing-eye dogs?"

"As a matter of fact, I do."

"What's his name?"

"Buck—named after the greatest dog there ever was."

"Greatest dog ever? I don't know, man. What about *Lassie*? I'd say *Lassie* is the greatest dog ever."

"The *Buck* I'm talking about makes *Lassie* look like a poodle. Don't you read? *Buck* is from *The Call of the Wild*. You ever have to read that in school?"

"I'm not sure." Mark scratched his head. "So why not bring Buck to the golf course with you?"

"That's why you're here."

"So, I'm doing the work of a dog?"

Vic's laugh was deep and he appeared amused. "I'll be happy if you're half as useful as Buck." Vic stood and felt around the tabletop. "Let's go out to the putting green." He found the cane and kept it collapsed in one hand while sticking out the free hand. "You mind guiding me the way?"

"Nah, just tell me what to do."

"Let me grab hold of your elbow."

Mark glanced around hoping no one was watching. *This is worse than being seen with Granny at the grocery store.* Mark pushed through the metal double doors.

Vic stumbled next to him. "I don't need too many warnings kid," Vic said, shaking his head. "But when I don't have the cane out, a little friendly warning of anything in my path is helpful. You know what I mean?"

"Oh man, sorry 'bout that," Mark felt his face flush. He slowed the pace. "Okay, two steps coming up."

"I assume you mean going down?"

"Yep. Sorry 'bout that. Two steps going down."

"I really hope this'll be fun for you." Vic slowed to a stop. "The only dirty part is when you have to replace my divots and fix my ball marks. But even that shouldn't be too bad."

"I guess."

"Oh, and of course, you'll have to help me out whenever I use the bathroom."

I knew this gig was too good to be true. Mark froze. *I should quit right now.*

"Hey kid, I'm just yanking your chain." Vic flashed a big smile. "It's a joke. I don't need no help in the can."

Mark took a deep breath. "Very funny."

"Lighten up." Vic gestured with a hand. "Get used to joking when you're around me. My golf bag should be in one of the stalls. It's brown. Check the tag."

"Got it." Mark grabbed the bag by the handle and eased his elbow into Vic's waiting hand. Paired together, and moving at a slow pace, it was as if they were nervously walking down a wedding aisle.

When they stopped, Vic said, "Stand the bag up here." He felt the tops of the clubs, grasped the putter, and pulled it out. "Let's start with a few putts." He drew three golf balls from his pocket and dropped them onto the turf. He pointed the grip-end of the putter like a magic wand. "Here you go."

Mark felt confused. "You want me to pull you around with the club?"

"No," Vic said. "Even though that's how we'll do it out on the course. What I want you to do is take a few putts."

"You want me to play?"

"Yeah."

"But I thought I was out here to help you."

"You are. I figured out a way I'd like us to get acquainted. Know what I mean? Now, place those three balls about five feet from the nearest cup."

"This ain't another joke."

"No joke, go ahead."

Mark did as he said. "Okay." Standing next to Vic on the green, he felt noticeable as a deer hunter dressed in bright orange. He looked around. At the clubhouse, he noticed the woman watching from a window. In another direction, a group of boys from his school lurked under a large tree. *They're going to start something. So...just ignore them.*

Vic spoke in the general direction of his target. "Okay, go ahead and try to make each putt." Dark shades covered his eyes.

Mark pulled back the putter and swung it forward. After the ball rolled past the hole, he looked back at Vic. "I missed the first one."

"I know."

The second ball clicked off the putter face.

"Aw," Vic said, shaking his head. "You missed that one too. Move in a little closer if you need to."

"C'mon man."

Mark hit the third putt.

It rattled into the bottom of the cup. Vic said, "*Magnifico!*"

Mark smiled. "You hear pretty good, huh?"

"Got to." Vic grinned.

Just then, Mark heard a high-pitched voice, "Tweet, tweet, here birdie, birdie." Alerted to the taunt, he swiveled his head in the direction of the loitering classmates. They appeared to be childlike, gazing innocently in random directions; cowards trying to hide in plain sight.

"Now, I want to try something else," Vic said, pointing in the air. "Did you know that some professionals practice putting with their eyes closed? It helps them to develop feel."

Ignore the punks. Mark turned to Vic. *Stay out of trouble.*

"Okay. Line up the same three balls again, and this time, I want you to close your eyes when you putt."

"Close my eyes?" *That's silly.* "You sure this ain't another joke?"

"Nah, nah."

Mark looked toward the hole, sat the blade behind the ball, closed his eyes, and swept the putter. He missed the first attempt, but made the second one. Each time he spent a little more time studying the situation before closing his eyes.

"How about that?" Vic nodded and smiled. "You made one out of three. Same as when you had your eyes open."

"It wasn't so hard."

"You're probably right about that." Vic raised his index finger. "But, I noticed you took a little more time with each putt. I assume you were lining yourself up. You were determining how hard you should swing. And finally, when you had all that information stored up, that's when you closed your eyes."

"That's about right."

Another jeer came from the distance, "Hey jail birdie, why aren't you wearing your stripes?"

Mark glared in the direction of the catcalls. The boys continued their innocent pretense. After a few seconds, when he felt they were looking in his direction, he turned his back, unfolded his middle finger, and waved it in the air.

"There's a reason I wanted you to try it with your eyes closed," Vic said. "I wanted you to understand what I'm going to need from you. I don't have the luxury of making all those calculations myself. That's where you come in."

"Doesn't sound too difficult."

"That's where you may be surprised my friend. A big part of my success depends on how good my information is. You know what I mean?"

"Still, doesn't sound all that hard."

"We'll find out soon enough. Now, let me give it a try. Set the balls out there for me."

Mark slapped the grip-end of the putter into Vic's open hand.

The high-pitched voice resounded. "Tweet, tweet, here birdie, birdie."

Vic held the putter in the air. "The *teppistas*—" He craned his neck. "Over there—"

"Who?"

"They bothering you?"

"Nah. How'd you know?"

"Remember kid, I'm not deaf."

Mark glanced over and noticed they were moving on. "They're walking away."

"They bothering you kid?"

"It's kind of a long story, man."

"Maybe you could tell it to me sometime."

"Maybe." Mark didn't like being an easy target for others. Doubts grew about being a coach for a blind golfer. "And while we're at it, why do you keep calling me kid? I'm almost eighteen years old."

"Hey, lighten up. It's a term of endearment—kind of like pal or buddy. I call everybody kid." Vic smiled. "We're here to have fun."

"I just wanted to make sure you knew how old I was, and that I can handle anybody picking on me. You see I'm on this timetable and I'm staying out of trouble."

"Like I said, I didn't mean anything by it." Vic looped the putter in the air. "The wise guys, they're gone?"

"Yeah."

"All right. So set me up so I can take a few putts."

Mark grabbed the end of the putter and pulled it towards the ground. "The ball is right in front of you. The hole is about five feet away."

"Okay, stand behind me." Vic stepped back and took a few practice swings of varying speed. "Watch how hard I'm swinging and tell me too much, too little, or just right."

"Little more. Little more. Little less. Okay, just right."

"Now place the putter on line for me behind the ball. Make sure my feet, shoulders, and putter blade are all lined at the target."

Mark bent down and placed the blade behind the ball. "Okay. Go ahead."

Vic drew back the club and made his stroke.

The ball fell over the lip and rattled in the cup.

Mark couldn't believe it. "You made it!"

"I know."

"And you're—" Mark stopped himself.

"Ah, *Marone*." Vic gathered his fingertips to its opposing thumb and stirred. "One day, you'll get it kid."

We're bored," said eight-year-old Terry Corvid.

"Yeah," echoed his seven-year-old brother, Corey.

"C'mon," Mark pulled open the kitchen door, "let's go outside." A wooden plank creaked as he stepped onto Granny's back porch. Mark claimed the lone chair as if it were his throne.

Terry followed by dusting off the top step and taking a seat.

Corey jumped to the ground stirring a pile of dust. He grabbed a stick and started thrashing at the weathered two-by-four handrail. He glanced up at Mark. "Tell us a story."

Mark leaned back. The slats of the chair groaned. *Perfect time for a little damage control.* Mark rubbed his chin and surveyed the backyard. He considered the leaky roof on the detached one-car garage and then looked over at the toppled concrete birdbath. He pointed towards the rear corner of the lot. "You see that broken board in the fence back there?" He swung his head to shake the stringy locks from his eyes. "Want to know how it got there?"

"Sure we do," said Terry, sporting an orange ring around his mouth from a Popsicle Granny had given him.

"If I tell you, you have to keep a secret, because the police don't like me for what happened there." Mark stuck out his hand. "Let's shake on it." His fingers swallowed each of the smaller hands. *No telling what they've overheard.* "In case either one of you think maybe I've been in trouble with the police, I figured both of you should know the *real* truth."

"I never heard anything," Corey said, returning to the bare patch. His mouth and tongue were tinted from a grape Popsicle.

"Just in case you do, I thought you should hear about it from me. You see, it all started when I was watching TV one afternoon." Mark pushed back in the chair as if a screen were in front of him. *I'll give 'em something they'll eat up.* "All the sudden the news people interrupted." Mark leaned forward. "I was kind of mad at first, because it was right at the best part of this show. But then I heard them say that a *lion* had escaped from the zoo."

Corey scratched his head and said, "A real lion?"

"Of course it was real." Mark expected more of a reaction. *Better sound convincing.* "Don't real lions live at the zoo?"

Corey kicked at the dirt and nodded.

"The TV reporters said, 'Let's go to our live cameras.' They showed this guy with a microphone. He was pointing at this empty cage."

"But how did it escape?" Terry looked up from the top step. "What did it look like?"

"Hold your horses." Mark pushed at the air. "I'm about to tell you. See, this little kid saw everything and the reporter was talking to him. He said the lion got a running start—" Mark wiggled two fingers like they were legs. "And got close a few times before he finally got up enough steam to make it all the way over. You see, whoever built the lion's cage made this huge concrete wall look like a jungle and figured no lion would ever get over it. I guess that old lion finally figured out that if he tried really hard, he could."

"Oh."

"So this kid—" Mark made his eyes bigger. "He looked like he was having trouble breathing. He said the lion escaped and was roaring at all the people."

"But don't they have zookeepers?"

"Oh, definitely, they do." Mark nodded. "But they must've been at lunch or something."

"Or what about a lion tamer?"

"He must've been at lunch too." Mark shrugged his shoulders. "Anyway, the man came back on the TV and started pointing at a map of the zoo. He said the lion ran by the monkey cages, and they just laughed. Then he ran by the giraffes, and they just kept on eating at the tops of these trees." Mark scratched like a monkey and stretched his neck for the giraffe. "Finally, the lion saw the front gate and made a run for it."

"But what about the people taking tickets, what did they do?"

"Nothing." Mark shook his head. "If you were safe in that booth, do you think you'd come out and step in front of a man-eating lion?"

"Um, I guess not."

"C'mon man. Of course you wouldn't. Anyway, about this time, the TV reporter said they had spotted the lion. You see, they had these helicopters in the sky looking for him."

"Did the lion bite anybody?"

"No, not yet. He was running down this street roaring at people—scaring 'em half out of their wits. But everyone definitely thought he would." Mark stood and shook out his long hair. "But listen, the pictures on TV started getting shaky because they were taken from this helicopter. At first I couldn't see the lion anywhere because of some trees. Then, they zoomed in, and there he was." Mark pointed. "I couldn't believe it, man."

Corey raised a hand as if he were in the classroom. "What'd he look like?"

"At first, it just looked like a brown furry ant because the helicopter was so high. But when they zoomed in, you could tell for sure that it was a lion. He was trotting down a street normal as the ice cream man. His big old head was covered with a dark-brown, furry mane and he was clomping on the pavement with his huge paws. When he roared, you could see every one of his sharp teeth." Mark stretched his lips to show his own teeth.

"I've never seen a real lion before," said Terry.

"You better hope you never have to." Mark nodded. "But let me get to the good part. See, about that time the sound of the helicopters seemed to be getting louder. I figured out why. It was because I could here them outside my window."

"No way," said Corey.

"Yes way, for sure." Mark nodded. "I looked out the window and saw one hovering up the block. I ran out the front door and when I looked back down the street, wouldn't you know it, here comes the lion."

"I don't believe it."

"Well, you better believe it." Mark nodded. "It was scary. See, once that lion saw me standing in the street, he got angry and roared. Then, he came charging right at me."

"What'd you do?"

"C'mon man, what'd you think I did?" Mark slapped Terry on the back. "I started running."

Both boys nodded in agreement all the while leaning closer and closer.

"I ran as fast I could toward the backyard." Mark stood. *I bet they never paid this much attention to any teacher.* "When I looked up, I saw the lion running down the side of my house. He rounded the corner and headed straight for me."

"What did you do?"

"See this chair?"

"Yeah."

"Well I grabbed it in one hand. I unfastened my belt and whipped it off." Mark lifted the chair. "I held this chair in front of me in one hand and I started slinging around the buckle-end of my belt. I slapped it to the ground and the lion stopped dead in his tracks."

"Then what?"

"I started backing him into the corner over there." Mark pointed to the backyard. "You see this knick in the leg of the chair?" Mark spread his curled fingers wide and pawed the leg. "That's where he took a swipe at me."

"No way," said Corey.

"Yes way. Look, you can see where his claw tore into the wood."

Terry appeared convinced. "It really is a claw mark."

"So, I trapped him over in that corner. And his breath stank." Mark waved his hand in front of his nose. "While I had that chair out in front of me and my belt whipping around, that old lion started roaring and swatting at me even more. He started kicking with his hind legs. As I was backing him into the fence, one of them kicks knocked out that board."

"No way."

"Yes way."

"Then what?"

"Next?"

"Yeah," said Terry. "What happened next?"

"Well you see, while I had him cornered there in the backyard, I could hear all the police sirens getting closer." Mark sat in the chair and rubbed his chin. "I heard the helicopter, but I couldn't see it anymore." Mark pointed to the sky. "But all of the sudden, this rifle shot blasted out. A dart with red feathers went flying through the air and stuck into the lion's rump."

"They shot 'em?"

"Yeah." Mark nodded. "Right in the bee-hind. But not with bullets. They hit him with a dart. It took two more darts before they finally got enough venom in him to take him down."

"They killed the lion?"

"No, no. They just put him to sleep. He was passed out cold. It took about ten people from the zoo to lift him and put him in the back of a wagon. I'm sure he slept the whole way back to the zoo."

"How did they wake him up?"

"I don't know." Mark shrugged his shoulders. "I didn't follow 'em back. But I can tell you, that later on, when I was watching the news, they had a picture of that lion back in his cage. He was running around on the inside like nothing had happened."

"Were you on the news?"

"Nah man, you see that's why the cops are mad at me." Mark looked off in the distance. "They went around telling everybody how they captured that lion. They took all the credit for it. They were on TV and everything. I think even the Mayor wanted to give them a medal or something. You see, the cops didn't want anybody to know that I was really the one that caught the lion. You see, they wanted to get all the glory and be the one shaking hands with the Mayor and stuff like that. And if they went and said it was really me that captured the lion, they wouldn't be able to do all that stuff." *See, I'm no degenerate.*

"But what about the helicopter? Didn't they see you capture the lion?"

"It must've been the trees. I think they blocked the view."

Mark's sister opened the back door and stepped out on the porch. Her arms were folded in front of her. "What are you boys doing?"

"I'm just telling them a story," Mark said.

"Well, it's time for us to go." She looked out into the backyard. "You two come inside and tell Granny goodbye."

When Mark arrived at the golf course for their practice session, Vic handed him a rectangular package that looked like a bundle from a laundry service. "Here," he said, "my wife put this together for you."

Mark untied the crisscrossing cord and ripped through the brown paper to find a stack of shirts. "What's this?"

"I hope you don't mind hand-me-downs. My wife went through my golf shirts and wanted to give you those. They should fit you fine. Pick one out and put it on."

"But I like what I'm wearing."

"Maybe so, but the *canottiera—*" Vic tightened his lips and rubbed his chin. "Look it kid, it might be okay to lie around your house in your underwear, but it ain't exactly appropriate for the golf course."

"C'mon, Vic. You can't even see what I'm wearing." Mark usually wore a tank top. It was the next best thing to going shirtless. He never thought about changing pants because everyone wore blue jeans. And the army boots, they made him feel taller. "What do you care?"

"It's not just about me."

Mark pulled a shirt from the stack and slid it over his head.

"Let me ask you something." Vic rested his hands on top of the golf bag. "You ever dress up for anything, you know, wear nice clothes?"

"C'mon, Vic. This another one of your jokes?"

"No. I'm just wondering."

"Man, I can't remember the last time." Mark's long hair swayed like a curtain as he shook his head. "Granny drug me to church once."

"That's it. That's what I'm asking."

"First my clothes, now you're pushing church?"

"No, no. When you went, did you wear something nice?"

"You mean like a coat and tie?"

"That, or either just something nicer than normal."

"Yeah, I guess so. It kept Granny from having a conniption."
Mark crossed his arms. "But after that, I made a deal with her—she couldn't drag me to church anymore."

"When you went inside the church, did you remain quiet when you were supposed to?"

"Of course." *He sounds like the case manager.* "I was on my best behavior." *I can give those same answers if that's what he wants.*

"That's it. That's the words I'm looking for. You were on your best behavior?"

"C'mon, Vic. I'm not a complete idiot."

"Well, I bring this up because ninety-nine percent of the people you see out here think of this place like church. I know it's a far stretch to call the grounds *sacred*—and that's not what I'm saying. But, the golf course is a place to be respected. You should follow the rules and be mindful of those around you. You know what I mean?"

"Man, just when I thought you were all right, you're starting to sound like a screw."

Vic shrugged his shoulders. "It's not too much to ask."

Initially, Mark thought to argue or protest, but decided it wasn't worth the effort. "Did I tell you about my timeline and how I'm supposed to stay out of trouble?"

"You mentioned it."

"Are you testing me, to see if I'm serious about it?"

"No," Vic said without hesitation. "I'm not here to test you on anything."

Mark liked Vic. And compared to picking up trash on the highway, the golf course had to be better. "I'm getting tired of all this practicing nonsense," Mark said, trying to change the subject. "When we going to get on the course?"

"I'm glad you asked. I thought we'd try a few holes today. I even arranged for us to take a cart."

"A golf cart?"

"Yeah, I got a key from Shorty." Vic pulled a key from his pocket and dangled it. "Usually we'll walk—the exercise is good for me. But today I'm a little short on time and thought we'd try riding a few holes. Go over and pick one out."

"You want me to get a golf cart?"

"You suggesting that I drive?"

Mark shrugged then snuck over to the waiting carts. He looked around, and then hopped in the furthest one from the clubhouse. He slipped the key in, turned it, tapped on the pedal, and rolled towards the practice putting green. He strapped Vic's bag to the rear frame, then guided him to the passenger seat. Mark then crept back around and slid behind the wheel. With the parking brake disengaged, he pressed the gas pedal. He steered with caution in the direction of the driving range.

For a long stretch, the only conversation involved the warm-up and swing instructions. It wasn't until Vic had a 7-iron in his hands that he broke the chain. "All this talk about church reminds me of this friend of mine," Vic said. "Have I told you about the *stronzo*?"

Mark placed the clubhead behind another ball and backed away. "You're clear."

Vic made another swing and connected with the range ball.

Mark placed another ball. "What's a *strunze*?"

"It's an Italian word." Vic stirred the air with his fingers. "Some day I'll tell you what it means. But for now, that's what we called this buddy of mine. Talking about church reminded me of the *stronzo*."

"He some kind of preacher?"

"No." Vic made another swing. "Not even close."

"Instead of saying 'I do', did he say 'I don't'?" Mark kicked another ball in place and set the club behind it. "You're clear."

"No, but you're getting closer. It did have something to do with a woman." Vic sent another practice ball flying. He propped his hands on the club like it was a walking stick. "You know how at some churches there comes a time when you're supposed to greet people around you and shake their hands?"

"I guess."

"Well, this one Sunday, when *Stronzo* takes his seat in the pew, he looks up, and right in front of him is this guy that he thought had been making the moves on his girlfriend. All these bad thoughts started swimming through his head. He started getting all steamed. And so, when it came time for everyone to shake hands, the *stronzo* ignored the guy. This poor schmuck stood there smiling with his hand stuck out. But the *stronzo* just glared and didn't shake his hand."

"He looked pretty dumb, huh?"

"I hope you're talking about the *stronzo*." Vic nodded. "Because, there, in God's house and all, it was not the time to be angry or even think about revenge or jealousy or anything like that."

"But was he dressed nice?"

"Don't be a *rompiscatole*." Vic flashed a wry smile. "The dress code's not part of this story. What made the *stronzo* an even bigger fool was when he found out later that the guy sitting in front of him wasn't even the right guy to be mad at. He got all nutty with anger and it was the wrong guy."

"Sounds like an innocent mistake."

"I'd say he made more than one mistake."

Mark placed another ball and backed away. "All clear."

Vic made another swing and sent another ball flying down the practice range. "That's enough. Let's try to play a few holes."

Mark guided Vic to the passenger seat, then walked around and sat behind the wheel. He hit the accelerator and headed around the clubhouse. As they passed a bench situated behind the first tee he lifted his foot from the gas. They glided past the empty trough that held golf balls to determine teeing order on crowded days before he pressed on the brakes. The engine fell silent. Mark hopped from the seat and rushed to the back of the cart.

"That must've been some covey of doves." Vic said, standing and holding onto the seatback. "How many were there, more than ten?"

"What?"

"Sounded like about ten."

"Birds? I didn't see any birds. How'd you know what kind they were?"

"Doves have a very distinctive sound—they kind of whistle when they take off." Vic whistled. "Kind of like that. You can even hear their wings beating the air when you jump 'em or they flare off in the air. I don't know of any other bird that sounds like that."

"That's weird, man."

"Weird? I like birds—they fascinate me. You may be surprised to know that birds are easy to identify by noise."

"I still say it's weird."

"Not me. I listen all the time. Mother Nature is a noisy place—Honking geese. Hawks screeching. Hammering woodpeckers. Trumpeting swans. And that's just of few of the flying objects."

"Whatever."

Mark listened, but could only hear the manmade roar of a gasoline engine. It grew louder as it approached from the maintenance shed. Mark turned to see the machinery come to a halt.

Oh no, here we go.

Luke Dengel smashed on the brake and sprang from the seat. "What are you doing on a golf cart?" Spittle flew as he growled.

Dread descended upon Mark. He thought about the worst-tasting medicine and had hoped to avoid a dose of Luke Dengel. Mark fumbled for words. He pointed to Vic and said, "I've got to drive."

"I don't care." Mirrored sunglasses covered Luke Dengel's eyes. His lip quivered and the striped muscles in his jaw twitched. "You're banned for life from ever riding, much-the-less driving one of my golf carts."

Mark held up both hands. If he had a white flag, he would've waved it too.

"It's okay." Vic raised both his hands. "That you Luke?"

Luke Dengel stopped glaring at Mark and appeared to calm. "Yeah," he said, "it's me."

"It's my fault the kid's driving," Vic said. "I told him to."

"*You* told him?"

"Yeah, we're only out to play a few holes and I cleared it with Shorty. It's not too crowded, so he thought it would be okay."

Mark kicked at the dirt. *Stupid old Dingleberry.*

Luke Dengel spit a stream of tobacco juice on the dusty path and removed his work gloves. "Shorty said it was okay?" Balled fists pressed against his hips.

"Yeah." Calmness remained in Vic's voice. "Go ask him if you need to. I think it's going to help with what we're doing here."

Luke Dengel stiffened and pointed at Mark. "I could care less what you're doing with this *good for nothing degenerate.*"

Vic twisted his head. "Aren't you being a little harsh?"

"A little harsh? Don't you know the story about this *worthless hoodlum*?"

"I'm aware of his past lapses in judgment."

"I'd call it more than a *lapse of judgment*," said Luke Dengel. Sweat seeped through the headband of his worn hat. "Did you know I was the one that discovered the whole mess?"

"We've never really talked about it." Vic shrugged his shoulders. "And I figured I didn't need any of the details."

Mark cringed. *If only the ground would open up and swallow him.*

"Well, you should." Luke Dengel waved a finger in the air. "First thing I spotted that morning was the door panel of the cart barn kicked out. The lock was busted. The carts inside looked like they come from a demolition derby—most of 'em total wrecks."

Vic maintained a calm expression. "I figured that was all in the past."

"Fiberglass side panels were cracked everywhere and front bumpers were smashed in." Luke Dengel continued as if he were talking to himself. "Tables were crushed and the ball washer was overturned. There were range balls everywhere. It looked like a tornado had hit the place. Obscene words painted everywhere. Used engine oil was dumped on the workbench—smelled like a gusher down in Texas. We're lucky the place didn't catch fire and burn to the ground.

"And that wasn't the worst of it." Luke Dengel spit another stream of tobacco juice, swallowed, and continued, "Once I noticed a few carts missing, I headed out to the course and noticed a mud bog had grown in the middle of the first fairway. Circling tire tracks made it a muddy mess.

"I looked over to the sand bunkers and noticed tire tracks there too. A herd of elephants couldn't have torn 'em up worse. But that was nothing compared to the putting green.

"The sprinklers must've softened 'em up. What a disaster. Circling ruts ripped into the Bermuda. If I look close enough, I can still see the tracks today. Yet, that's not the worst of it.

"What really broke my heart is when I finally spotted the missing golf carts. I couldn't believe it. Only the tops of 'em was visible." Luke Dengel shook his head. "Two of 'em submerged to the steering wheel. The little joyride wasn't enough. They had to go and drown 'em.

"After the police made their report, the boys towed 'em out and spent a week scraping off goop and rebuilding engines. So, you'll have to excuse me if you think I'm being a little too harsh."

Vic remained like a statue. Although his sunglasses covered his eyes, he appeared to be looking off in the distance.

"You should know this much." Luke Dengel raised a finger in the air. "This *no-good piece of cow dung* you've got helping you around ain't that smart." He took off his hat and wiped his brow. "The same muddy tracks that lead me around the golf course were easy to follow." Luke Dengel pointed a finger at Mark. "The cops traced them to the back of his house."

Mark started to say something but stopped. Nothing he could say would ever soothe Luke Dengel.

"I know you weren't alone—birds of a feather." Luke spat then hopped back onto his work cart. "You never did come clean. There were just too many footprints, and more than one cart swamped in the pond. We'll find out who was with you." He pumped the gas pedal, turned the key, and sped off.

Mark let out his breath and slumped over the steering wheel.

Vic finally broke the silence. "We ready?"

"You're not going to ask me about all the details?"

"That's up to you. That's your business."

"I didn't have much to do with all those things he said. It was other people."

"I believe you."

"You want to know who they were?"

"That's up to you."

"You don't want to know what happened?"

"Like I said, that was in the past. You got a fresh start with me. But I can understand why Luke might be a little angry about the whole thing."

"Yeah, but why's that dude always dumping a load of grief on me? It's getting old."

"Give him time."

Stupid old Dingleberry.

WEEK SIX

The case manager reclined behind the desk with his fingers interlocked behind his head. "So—" he said, rocking slowly. "How are things going with Mr. Adano?"

Mark twirled a capped pen on the desktop like it was a board game spinner. "All right, I guess."

"You can always switch to highway litter."

"If you put it that way." Mark squirmed higher. "It's going great. We're spending most of the time practicing. It's kind of boring setting up one shot after another." He looked across the desk. "It would really be better if I got to play too."

"Don't even bring it up." The case manager stopped rocking. "You're not there for yourself. You're there to help someone else. I don't mean to clip your wings, but playing golf alongside Mr. Adano is out of the question."

"Hey man, I just thought it might help."

"Like I said, it's out of the question. Better yet—" The case manager's fingers drew quotation marks in the air. "To use a golf term—consider the idea 'out of bounds.'"

"I was only trying to help." Mark shrugged his shoulders. *Why can't he see that?*

"Let's move on. What's on your mind?"

Being misunderstood only frustrated Mark. He furrowed his brow. "You know how I told you about this guy, Luke Dengel?"

"That's someone from the golf course?"

"Yeah, well, he needs to lay off me."

"Is there a problem?"

"I think so. The dude's always hassling me."

"Do you have any specific examples?"

"Yeah, he's always yelling at me."

"Anything more specific than that?"

Mark thought for a while. "Yeah, he said he was going to stuff a shirt full of hay and hang it in a tree behind my house." Mark raised a hand in the air. "He said it was going to be a scarecrow and it was supposed to keep me off his golf course."

"He really said that?"

"Yeah man. And it's not just me. I think he has it out for the whole neighborhood." Mark slumped in his seat. "That reminds me of something else." He stared at the ceiling and then at the clock.

"Go on."

"It was yesterday, when I was walking home. I did something stupid."

"What was it?"

Mark eased an elbow onto the desk. "For more than a year now, I've been kind of avoiding certain people."

"We've talked about that."

"Well, finally, I ran into 'em, and like I said—"

"Go on."

"I was coming back from the store. And lately, I've been taking a different route. Yesterday, I must've been in a hurry, or just not paying attention. Just when I walked by the McMurtry's house, I heard, 'Hey Crowbar', and I thought how stupid I was."

"What did you do?"

"What could I do? I slowed down and looked towards the porch. Moose was standing there. He said, 'Whatcha got in the bag?' And I said, 'Hey man, it's something for Granny.' You see, that's why I had gone to the store. Anyway, Moose waved, 'Come on up. I hadn't seen you in a while.' So, what could I do? I stepped around all the junk in their front yard and put a foot up on their bottom step."

"Remind me, why is it that you've been 'avoiding' this Moose?"

"Well, you see, whenever I'm around Moose and Skeeter, trouble seems to follow me around." Mark paused for a while. "And you know about the timeline, and how I'm staying out of trouble."

The case manager nodded. "Go ahead."

"Don't you have to keep the stuff I tell you secret?"

"Generally, yes."

"C'mon. I'd say you need to swear it."

"Okay, I give you my word," said Mr. Shannon, raising a hand like a Boy Scout taking a pledge. "I promise that nothing you ever say will be told to anyone else without your permission. That fair?"

"I guess." Mark didn't trust him completely, but decided to go on with the story anyway. "You see, when I first moved into the neighborhood, there weren't any other kids around. Skeeter's the little brother. Moose is older. At first, I think they just had fun picking on me. Moose would start teasing me. Then Skeeter would join in. They wouldn't let me go home until I'd fight Skeeter on their front lawn. They called it the 'Cage of Bravery'. I couldn't chicken out. Moose acted like a referee, but I could swear there was a few times he got in punches of his own." Mark looked over to the case manager to gauge his reaction.

Mr. Shannon nodded. "You got into fights with them, they threw punches at you, but you still remained friends?"

"Like I said, there wasn't anyone else around. I figured I could eventually get them to like me. And anyway, once I started getting bigger than Skeeter, we stopped having the cage matches."

"Then you felt like they were your friends?"

"I guess. But they started talking about these 'Tests of Manhood.' They said there was a list of things I had to do to be like them."

"What kind of tests?"

"Stupid stuff mainly. I remember one of them. It was me climbing up a ladder. I had to grab this tree branch, and then they took the ladder away. I had to hang for thirty minutes before they would give back the ladder."

"That doesn't sound like fun."

"It wasn't."

"And you agreed to do it?"

"Yeah man, I guess I wasn't so smart then." Mark nodded and hung his head. The long hair covered his face. "But let me get back to Moose. He said, 'How come you haven't been by to see us?' I just acted like I had been busy with other stuff. 'You want a beer?' he said to me, then he yelled into the house, 'Hey, Skeeter. Bring me out another beer.' He just stood there waiting for his beer. Finally, he got to the point of what he was wanting to ask me. He said, 'So, how was your time behind bars?'

"I just acted like it was no big deal.

"Then he said, 'You did right by not squealing.'

"I kinda just nodded.

"Then he said, 'Me and Skeeter was real proud of you. We even wanted to throw you some kind of party when you got back home.' Then he opened his front door and yelled inside, 'Hey Skeeter! Come look and see who's come to visit.'"

The case manager patted his beard. "So, they knew why you got in trouble?"

"Yeah. Now I'm not saying anything else, you understand?"

"I understand."

"Besides, you promised."

"You have my word."

"So Skeeter comes pouring out of the house and practically jumps on my back. After he gave me a few little swipes he settled down. 'How was prison you old jailbird?' he says to me.

"And I just said it was okay and all.

"Then he said, 'We knew you'd never squeal. We knew you knew better,' he said.

"And I just nodded.

"Then he lifted his shirt and showed me this pistol stuck in his pants."

Mr. Shannon stopped scribbling his notes and looked up. "A gun?"

"Sure. He said, 'Check this out Crowbar. I picked this up for fifty bucks.' He waved it around.

"Now I ain't saying he ever pointed it at me, but I kind of got a message. So I said, 'hey man, I've seen one like that before.' I didn't stick around long after that, being on my timeline and all. So I said I'd see 'em around."

Mr. Shannon sat in silence.

Is he waiting for more? "That's it," Mark finally said. *Is he ignoring me?* "And I got something else for you."

"What's that?"

"You remember how we always talk about my 'perfect dad' and all?"

"I recall some discussions along that line."

"Well, I've been thinking." Mark curled his upper lip and nodded. "Did you see that show the other night about this daredevil that jumps over stuff on his motorcycle?"

"No, I must've missed that one."

"Well, you missed something all right." Mark nodded. "They had this daredevil on TV jumping over a long line of school busses. There must have been fifteen of 'em. And man, he was popping wheelies and riding around while standing up on the seat. He was wearing this red, white, and blue uniform and a cape that was blowing behind him. His motorcycle was painted the same colors and roared every time he gave it the gas. Before it was time for him to soar over them busses, he zipped back and forth in front of the crowd doing tricks and waving."

"Sounds exciting."

"Oh man, it was." Long locks of hair swung as Mark nodded. "They even replayed a previous jump of his over a water fountain out in Las Vegas. It didn't turn out too good—he crashed at the end. They kept showing it over and over in slow motion—him bouncing off that bike."

"I think I know who you are talking about."

"Well, I figured it out and I think he'd be my perfect dad. He's got to be about the bravest guy in the world to keep getting on that motorcycle even though he's broken about every bone in his body." Mark glanced up. "Man, I could travel all around the world and learn how to pop wheelies on a motorcycle. I want to become a motorcycle daredevil."

"That would be ideal for you?"

"Yeah man." Mark put a finger in the air. "And my perfect dad would be Evel Kneivel."

WEEK SEVEN

"Worse score in years, *Molto brutto*," Vic said, after hearing the tally. He gestured with a hand. "Funny thing is—I don't feel like I was playing all that bad."

"C'mon, Vic." Mark looked over to the clock above the concession stand counter. He had logged a full day, and was ready to head home. "You did okay. Don't make me repeat 'em again."

"That's just it. I thought I was a little better than okay. Know what I mean?"

Mark felt a pang of guilt. This time he did know what Vic meant. He fiddled with the napkin holder atop the table and sank into his chair. *Maybe Vic is onto me?*

"The third hole, it seemed to all start going downhill on the third hole." Vic touched each of his fingers to his thumb. "You said I took an eight?"

"I don't remember. But that's what the scorecard says." Mark tried a little flattery to move Vic from the subject. "You played pretty good, I think."

"I've never made an eight on the third hole."

Mark thought back. *Is that where it started?*

"It felt good off the tee, but you said it went left."

"I don't remember."

"You said the next shot went too far right."

"I still don't remember."

"The next one came up short, and when I finally made it on the green, I missed four putts in a row."

"Yeah, Vic." Mark feigned a laugh. "You had some pretty bad luck on that one."

"I just don't understand it. I never four-putt."

Kinda funny at the time. Bored. Aiming him in the wrong direction. Just messing around. Telling him to hit it too hard. I'm in charge here. Who's laughing now? I'm caught. Mark tried to deflect any suspicions. "Why do you even care?"

"Why do I care?"

"Yeah. Why do you *even* care about golf?"

Vic leaned back and took a deep breath. "I guess nobody's ever asked me that before. If I had to really think about it—" He scratched his head, "I'd have to say that golf helped me get better. You know, after the accident." Vic touched at his face. "I spent a lot of time laying around feeling sorry for myself.

"One day Angela said, 'Stick out your hand.'

"I didn't know what she was doing, but she slapped a golf club in my palm and said my brother was on the way over to take me to the park to hit golf balls.

"I kind of laughed. I thought it was some kind of joke. When I realized she was serious, I figured I'd go just to humor her. But when we got there, my brother handed me the old driver and told me it wasn't a joke.

"I agreed to take a few swings. Eventually he teed up a ball for me. It took a few tries, but I finally caught one solid. I thought if I could do it once, with a little practice, I should be able to do it more often.

"So I did.

"Golf helped me realize that with a little practice, I could still do many things."

Mark was still worried about being caught. He tried to shift gears completely. He looked over at the concession stand grill. Steam from sizzling patties sidestepped the exhaust hood and traveled to their table. "I bet you really like pizza."

Vic turned his head. "Doesn't everybody?"

"I guess." Mark tapped the tabletop. "I bet you Italians like it better than hamburgers."

"I like hamburgers." Vic nodded. "And don't get me wrong, I like my Italian food. Lasagna, tortellini, linguine, baked ziti, and there's chicken, veal, and eggplant parmigiana, and there's calzone, stromboli, and cannelloni." Vic rubbed his belly. "Don't even get me started on the sauces. You name it, kid, I like it."

"You sound like a menu. I never hearda half that stuff."

"You don't know what you're missing. I'm getting hungry just thinking about it."

Mark smiled. After a few seconds, he said, "Your wife's never late."

"I think maybe we finished a little early. What time is it?"

"Three-thirty."

"Yeah, she said it would be closer to four. You don't have to wait."

Mark thought about splitting, but changed his mind. "I got nothing else to do."

Vic shrugged his shoulders. "So, what else is new? How's school?"

"Okay."

"Afternoons and weekends working out for you? Anything at school keeping you?"

"Nah."

"No sports or anything like that?"

"Nah."

"Don't you go to football games?"

"Never been. Full of losers acting like they're better than everyone else."

"What about dances?"

"Never been."

"You're missing out on things you'll never get a chance to do again."

"So what."

"You got a girlfriend?"

"C'mon, Vic." Mark tried to redirect the conversation. "What's with all the questions?"

"Just passing time—that's all. Trying to get to know you a little better."

"Oh."

"So, no girlfriend?"

"Not really. But I do like bird-dogging babes. No offense, but that's one thing you're missing."

Vic pressed the palms of his hands together as if he were praying, then swiveled them with each word. "You'd be surprised how much I can see."

"There ain't nothing better than scoping chicks."

"Scoping chicks? So *sciocco*…You've got a lot to learn my friend. When I had my sight, I noticed many women that were beautiful on the outside, but soon found out they were nothing but ugly ducklings on the inside."

"If you remember who they were, send 'em my way."

"You go out on dates?"

"A few. But it's been awhile. Let's just say I've been away on a forced vacation."

"It was like a vacation?"

"Not really. Not sure why I'd call it that. Sometimes I call it boot camp. Maybe it just sounds better."

"Okay. So tell me about your last date."

"It was with this chick named Linda." Mark glanced at the clock again.

"And how'd you meet?"

"We sat next to each other in Spanish class. We traded some stupid Spanish words back and forth and laughed at how funny they sounded. She even wrote me a note once using Spanish words. It was kind of funny. Anyway, we rode home on the same bus. She was always nice to me."

"Sounds pretty nice."

"Only one problem—she had a boyfriend. She was going with this dude since grade school. And if you ever saw him, you probably wouldn't think too much. You see, he's really not that tall and kind of skinny."

"They were kind of a mismatch?"

"Well, that's just the thing. See, Linda is real popular. Lots of guys would probably ask her out if it weren't for the boyfriend. But, everybody steers clear. Whether it's true or not, there are these rumors about him being a *Jujitsu* or *Karate* expert—or maybe it's *Tae Kwon Do*? He's always getting this crazy look whenever they're broken up. It's a daze, like he's been sniffing something, man. People think he's just ready to go off any second if anybody says anything about Linda or even goes near her."

"But it didn't stop you?"

"That's the thing, see. When we went out on a date they were broken up. And besides that, like these other girls kept telling me, she wanted to go out. So what could I do? I had to ask her out."

"But you also wanted to go."

"A smoking-hot babe like Linda? Who wouldn't?"

"Okay. So how'd it go?"

"I got my license about two months before—but I didn't drive much. I talked Granny into letting me use the car. I think it was about only the third time she ever did that. So, I picked up Linda and we went to a movie and then to this place for pizza. It was kind of late when we got back to her house, but she invited me inside."

"*Bravissimo.*"

"I know, man." Mark smiled and nodded. "So we sat in front of the TV—even though it was turned off. Her mom stayed in the kitchen while we sat on the floor looking at this photo album. Linda wanted to show me all these pictures of when she was a baby. It was nice.

"Finally, her mom said it was time for bed. Linda looked a little disappointed, but told her mom I was leaving. I moved toward the front door and thought about kissing her goodnight and all, but I wasn't sure if I should. She was kind of leaning on the edge of the door, and I was kind of standing in the doorway. Not wanting to do anything wrong, I just smiled and said, 'See you around.' She smiled back and thanked me for taking her to the movies. She closed the door and I walked to the street."

"Sounds like a pretty good night."

"Well that's just half of it. That's when things turned bad. You see, I looked up, and I saw her old boyfriend, the *Karate* expert, parked behind Granny's car. His motor was running. He rolled down his window."

"I tried to ignore him."

"He said, 'Come here! I want to talk to you.'"

"But I acted like I didn't hear him or anything. I jumped in Granny's car. Even though I was only going down the street, I started driving real fast.

"I decided I better try to lose him before he could find out where I lived. I sped right by Granny's house and took a right turn. I was flying. Mailboxes were zooming past. I looked in the rearview mirror, and there he was, right on my tail. I must've done three or four laps around the block before I decided I couldn't shake him. So, I pulled in Granny's driveway and hopped out of the car.

"I heard him again, 'Hey! I want to talk to you.'"

"I just kept on walking, a little faster now, until I got inside."

"So you made it home safe?"

"Yeah, but I looked out the curtains and saw him roaring the engine right in front of Granny's house."

"Did you call the police?"

"No, I never thought of that. But, I will have to admit, I was a little nervous, maybe even a little scared. I was thinking—what could I do against a *Jujitsu* expert?"

"What did you do?"

"I thought of only one thing—the pistol Granny keeps on her nightstand. I stopped outside her door and said, 'I'm home.' When she didn't say anything, I peeked inside and noticed she had fallen asleep. I saw the pistol. I lifted it off the table, and stuffed it in my pocket. I walked to the curtains, looked out in the street, and saw him still sitting in the car with the engine running."

"Ah *Marone*. I don't like where this is going."

"Well, I'm telling you the truth. And just hold on, see, I figured this dude wasn't going to leave, so I walked outside to the driveway and stood there.

"He rolled down the window a little further and said, 'Come here.'

"But I said, 'Hey man, you come here.'

"He said, 'I just want to talk to you.'

"I gripped the pistol. 'If you want to talk, you come here,' I said.

"I don't know if he saw the gun in my hand or not, but eventually he just drove away."

"Thank goodness for that," Vic said, shaking his head.

"I think about that night all the time."

"What about Linda?"

"I sometimes wonder if she ever found out about it." Mark shook his head. "I decided to play it cool and stayed away. A few weeks later I heard they were back together. I saw the dude at school after that and he said, 'Hey man, sorry about that night. I was kind of going crazy.' But I know if he weren't back with Linda he would've never said anything to me."

Vic's wife suddenly appeared. "I hope I'm not interrupting anything," she said. She leaned over the back of Vic's chair, wrapped her arms around his neck, and then kissed him on the cheek.

"Not at all." Vic was beaming. "Just a little man talk."

She tugged at Mark's sleeve. "That shirt looks good on you."

"Thanks." Mark smiled and stood. "I don't get as many dirty looks around here."

"I told you she has good taste," Vic said. "And, you should taste her *marinara* sauce."

"Hey Vic—" Mark nodded his head. "You were right. You did play pretty good today. You should've had a better score. I guess I could've done a better job."

"Forget about it kid." Vic raised a hand. "*Ciao.*"

"Chow?"

Vic smiled. "We'll get 'em next time."

Week Eight

With the shades pulled, a glow from the console was the only source of light in the room. Shifting colors danced on all the surfaces facing the screen. Outside, a diesel engine roared as a city bus departed on schedule from a nearby stop. On the television, Gomer Pyle was so full of surprises, he kept repeating the word. Sergeant Carter didn't like surprises; they boiled his blood and moved him closer to the brink of hysteria. Only a commercial break would prevent his total meltdown.

Mark sat next to Granny on the sofa. "I made a birdie today."

"I was wondering where you were."

"Don't you remember?"

Granny looked puzzled and shook her head.

"I told you last night."

"All I can remember dear is that you said, 'Good night.'"

"I said that, but right before that, I told you I'd be over at the golf course today. You remember?"

"Maybe."

On the screen, a man wearing a suit of leaves with his skin painted green stood in a miniature field holding a can of vegetables. He was saying the same thing as Santa Claus.

"I told you how they let me out of school early on Thursdays. You know, to get to the golf course on time. Remember now?"

"Oh yeah." She didn't appear very convinced.

"Anyway, I made a birdie today." Mark looked over at Granny. "You should've seen it."

"Oh, that's wonderful," said Granny, smiling. "I think I remember now."

"It was on a par-3. I punched a nice little 9-iron within three feet of the hole."

"Pappy would be so proud."

"I wish he could've been there."

"I got a feeling he's always watching over us."

Gomer's sheepish grin returned to the screen. It seemed to repel the verbal assaults from Sergeant Carter; especially when

Gomer knocked over a bucket of mop water. Mark saw a look of concern on Granny's face. She always liked Gomer, and hated when he got in trouble.

"Did my mom call today?"

"Not today dear."

"That reminds me of something." Mark rose from the sofa and went to his room. He dug into a zippered compartment of the golf bag and returned to the den. "I was cleaning out some stuff and found this." He handed over a folded newspaper clipping.

Granny unfolded the yellowed paper. "I haven't seen this in years. Where'd you find it?"

"In my golf bag."

"Pappy must have stuffed it in there. It's about his retirement. Look how young he is in that uniform." Granny touched the smile on the face in the picture. "And look at all the medals."

In the background, a commercial jingle claimed you could trust your car to the man that wears a star.

"How come you don't have this picture in a frame?"

"Oh, you know how your Pappy was when it came to bragging and boasting." Granny's voice was shaky. "He always gave credit to others. He always said he couldn't accomplish anything without a lot of good people around him. He gave such a wonderful speech at the retirement dinner."

"Where was I?"

"Why I can't even remember if you were born yet." The question appeared to catch Granny off guard and send her mind wandering. "Let me think."

"I was probably just a baby." Mark attempted to shorten her trip through time. "I don't even know if my sister was there. Maybe she once talked about not being able to go or having to stay home with a babysitter or something."

"That's funny," Granny said. "I can't remember if your mother was even at the party."

"Oh, I'm sure she was. Anyway, tell me about it."

"Pappy sure grabbed a hold of retirement," Granny said. "You never saw anybody get on with something like your Pappy. He swore he'd never sit around and talk about the old days. He took that bag of clubs over to Short Hills, and said he was going to get a fresh start of making new memories. Those golf clubs are what he got for a retirement present. Did you know that?"

"No. I didn't."

"Why don't you ever use the pushcart that goes with it?"

"It's broken."

"Broken?"

"Yeah, one of the wheels came off. I tried to fix it, but it wouldn't work."

Mark remembered what really happened. He and Skeeter decided to build a coaster cart. They searched the neighborhood for parts, and found two-by-fours and a triangular piece of plywood at a construction site. Skeeter found an old seat cushion from a fishing boat and unscrewed two small wheels from the back of a tricycle. Mark contributed two larger wheels after hijacking them from Pappy's idle golf pull cart.

"That's a shame." Granny turned back to watch Gomer stumble over an obstacle course wall. Sergeant Carter was screaming at him.

Mark thought about Pappy. "You remember that baseball uniform Pappy gave me when I was little?"

"What's that dear?"

"That baseball uniform."

"Wasn't that pajamas?"

To his surprise, Sergeant Carter discovered Gomer's bumbling had actually saved the day. The Marine Corp band played and the credits marched from the top of the screen.

"No. It was a real baseball uniform. It was the greatest birthday present I ever got. Pappy gave it to me. It was real heavy-duty wool, and all the edges were trimmed with red flannel. It buttoned in the front, and was exactly like a real major league uniform—only smaller."

"I do remember. I think Pappy got it at the sporting goods store."

"Well it was just about the best thing I ever had. I think I wore that baseball uniform everywhere."

"Yes, you did wear it everywhere."

"That's what I remember best about Pappy. That, and the fact that he used to let me take pictures with his camera."

"What's that dear?"

"Pappy's camera. He used to let me take pictures. No one else ever let me touch anything. I always got my hand slapped whenever I touched anything that could break easily. But, not Pappy. He treated me like a decent person. He let me touch stuff I wasn't supposed to. I remember how he used to get a big kick out of letting me push the button on that camera. I couldn't even see through the thing, but he let me push the button. Everyone else was saying, 'Oh, he'll break it', or 'Oh, you're wasting film', but not Pappy. He just laughed and let me have fun."

"I guess you're old enough now, and Lord knows, now that he's gone, I can tell you this—" Granny turned misty-eyed. "If it weren't for your Pappy, you and your sister would have had some disappointing Christmas mornings."

"Really?"

"Oh yes." She nodded. "It was Pappy that made sure your tree was filled with presents. Some years he went a little overboard. He always said we'd manage somehow."

Mountain music poured from the television. Uncle Jed was shooting at some food.

WEEK NINE

Listen kid—" Vic stood in taller grass that collared the putting green. "I've got to ask you something."

Vic's change in demeanor surprised Mark. *Here we go. He's had time to think. Now he wants the dirty details.* Mark looked to the ground. "Wha...what is it?"

Vic bent over and felt the tops of the blades. "How close am I to the green?"

"Another few feet ahead of you."

Vic continued feeling the turf until he reached the low-shaven surface. He stood and gripped the club. "Don't take this the wrong way, but I've got some suspicions."

I knew it. Vic was just like everybody else—the cops, boot camp goons, case managers, and stupid old Dingleberry.

"I'm not accusing you of anything, but I'd like to know."

Mark stooped and placed the club behind the ball. "Little more to the left." He tried to act normal. "Good."

Vic chipped the ball onto the green. When it stopped rolling, he grimaced. "You see, sometimes I get the feeling you're moving my ball around. Know what I mean?"

Mark felt puzzled and relieved. "That's it?"

"Yeah, like I said, I'm not accusing you of anything, but it seems like I've never had to hit from any trouble." Vic shrugged with palms up. "Come to think of it, since we've been together, I can't remember if I've ever had to count a penalty stroke."

"Heck Vic, if that's all you wanted to know, sure, I've been kinda moving you into a better spot every now and then." Mark took a deep breath. "I didn't think it was a big deal. I was only trying to help."

"Like I said, I didn't want to say anything—" Vic placed his right hand over his heart. "But I have to turn in my scores to keep an accurate handicap."

"If you knew I was doing it, you should've said something."

"That's why I'm saying something now. How 'bout this—" Vic rubbed his chin. "When we're approaching the next shot, you tell

me exactly where the ball's at—no matter what the situation. Don't
move it anywhere unless I give you the go-ahead."

"No problem." Mark ran his fingers through his hair. "Tell
me again why it's so important."

"To calculate my handicap—I turn in my score after every
round. If I don't follow the rules, I'm not doing myself, not to
mention any future partners or competitors, any favors."

"I see." Mark wasn't exactly clear. He was just happy Vic
hadn't brought up his tainted past. "Oops, I didn't mean to be funny."

"Look, I say 'see' and 'look' and 'watch' all the time." Vic
gestured with both hands. "It doesn't bother me when other people
say it too. What I can't stand is when someone brags about having a
low handicap when it's not for real."

"You're a real stickler."

"I guess I've learned to be. Not following the rules can be
embarrassing." Vic grabbed the handle on the pull cart. "You know
my old pal, *stronzo*?"

"I remember."

"Well, the old *stronzo* was the fourth man on our high school
golf team. His senior year, they made it to the regional tournament.
He was playing pretty well up to the thirteenth hole. But that's when
things fell apart."

"Let me guess—" Mark placed a club in Vic's hand and the
two of them started walking down the fairway. "Somebody moved his
ball and didn't tell him."

"Good guess." Vic smiled. "But that's not it. You see, it was
the day before when the worst thing happened to the *stronzo*. He went
out and played a practice round and shot the best score of his life—a
seventy-eight. So, the next day, when the score was going to count, he
thought he'd be able to shoot another seventy-eight. Well, that didn't
exactly happen. He started losing his cool early, and by the time he
made it to the thirteenth green, he could hardly control his emotions
any longer. He had a short putt—less than a foot for a bogey. Well, of
course he missed it."

Mark shrugged his shoulders. "It happens."

"Yeah, but this is the part where he really blows it." Vic
stopped walking. "The *stronzo* was so mad about missing the short
putt and not being able to repeat that seventy-eight, he reached down

and picked up the golf ball without finishing the hole. It was like he was putting himself out of misery. Well, long story short, he was disqualified. And since his score didn't count, his team's score didn't count either. It was a good thing they weren't in contention, or it would have really been a kick in the pants."

"From here out," Mark said, "I'll make sure we follow the rules."

"Deal."

Two holes later, Mark spotted Vic's ball in trouble. "I got some bad news for you."

"Are we out of bounds?"

"No, I can still see your ball."

"That doesn't actually decide whether it's out-of-bounds or not." Vic pointed in all directions. "Any white stakes marking the area?"

"I don't see any, but that's not the problem. Your ball is up against a tree."

"And there's no way I can swing at it."

"Not unless you want to smash your club." Mark looked back towards the tee. "And Vic, I got more bad news."

"What's that?"

"You know how you're always paranoid and asking me if anyone's behind us? Well, there's a group that looks like they're waiting for us to get moving."

"No problem—just wave 'em forward."

Mark signaled to the group then turned back to Vic. "Let's go over there."

"Remember kid, you've got to be a little more specific."

"Oh yeah, I even pointed. There's some trees on the other side. Let's wait in the shade."

"Now that sounds like a plan." Vic stuck out an elbow.

Once outside the fairway, Mark glanced back and noticed the group teeing off.

Vic said, "Now that we're here, let's take a look at the rule book."

"Rule book?"

"Yeah, check inside my bag, behind the long zipper."

Mark dug into the bag and pulled out the booklet. "Got it."

"Now thumb through there and tell me what it says."

It didn't take long for Mark to realize that he was in real trouble. The Roman numerals and definitions were alien as markings on a pyramid. He flipped through the pages and tried to change the subject. "Why don't you have a book with bumps and dots so you can read it with your fingers?"

"That's a good question," Vic said. He took off his sunglasses, wiped his face with a towel, and then put them back on. "But for that to happen, it wouldn't fit so easily in my golf bag. I carry the smaller version around expecting my coach to be able to read it. Know what I mean?"

"Oh." Mark rifled through the pages, but was lost. Two minutes passed before he finally said, "C'mon Vic, you really need this?"

"Yeah."

Mark let out a deep breath and confessed. "Well, you see, I'm not very good at this."

"No problem kid, I can help you through it. Flip to the index and look for something describing an unplayable lie."

"Index?"

"Yeah, the last few pages. Everything should be in alphabetical order."

Mark turned to the back of the booklet and searched down the list. "I got something here called 'Unplayable Ball'."

"That should be it. Go to those pages and read it to me."

Mark grew nervous again. He wanted to be helpful, but knew his limitations. "I ain't such a good reader Vic."

"Doesn't matter. I'll help you out."

"Thee—player—may—de—clair—his—ball—un—play—uble—at—any—place—on—thee—course—ex—sept—when—thee—ball—is—in—aigh—water—hazz—ard."

Out in the fairway, the group took their shots and waved thanks.

"I'll take the one-stroke penalty and drop one," Vic said.

Mark helped with measuring two club lengths, and then watched as Vic dropped a ball. After Vic took the shot, they walked toward the green.

"It's a good idea to carry that rule book for just such occasions," Vic said. "It's never a bad thing to know what you're talking about. That reminds me of another story about the *stronzo*. This one involves turkey potpie."

"Another story?"

"For some reason, he's always on my mind." Vic clucked. "Anyway, me and the *stronzo* went to get a bite to eat at a diner."

"You going to tell me what that word means?"

"Someday." Vic nodded his head and held a finger in the air. "Anyway, the *stronzo*, was trying to be funny with the waitress, but she wasn't in much of a joking mood. So my buddy orders the turkey potpie and he says to the waitress, 'Make that turkey potpie à la mode.' She gave him a funny look and said, 'Sir we don't serve turkey potpie à la mode.' But he was acting like he knew all about it and said to her, 'Well, that's the way I like mine.' So she brings us our food and puts this plate of turkey potpie in front of my buddy and it's got two scoops of vanilla ice cream on top."

"Ice cream?"

"Yep. So the *stronzo*, says, 'What's this?'

"And the waitress said, 'That's what you ordered.' Then she raised her nose in the air and said, 'I was in no mood to argue with such a refined gentlemen as yourself. Who am I to doubt your exquisite tastes?'

"My buddy frowned and started eating. I just knew it didn't taste very good. Once we got outside, it was time for him to eat some crow. He admitted he didn't know what 'à la mode' meant. He thought it meant bring it fast. He heard people order apple pie à la mode and thought they were saying something like 'on the double' or 'make it snappy.' He wanted to sound fancy, but he didn't actually know what he was talking about."

"So, à la mode means add ice cream?"

"Knowing what you're talking about before you open your trap reminded me of that story." Vic smiled and raised a finger in the air. "So don't go ordering turkey potpie à la mode."

After staring at the green fuzzy coating for more than a few minutes, Mark could no longer resist. He had to feel it. He reached into the wire basket and grabbed the tennis ball. He held it near his nose to let the synthetic gasses register in his brain. He began tossing it in the air. "What's this for?"

"Someone gave me the idea to squeeze it during the day to help get rid of stress," Mr. Shannon, the case manager said. "If you had two more, you'd actually be juggling."

"You don't like my tricks with one?" Mark tried unsuccessfully to spin it on a fingertip like a basketball.

"Doesn't seem all that challenging."

"C'mon man. I could join the circus." He lobbed the ball toward his bicep, snapped his arm straight to pop the ball in the air, and then caught it with the same hand.

"If you say so." The case manager leaned forward.

Mark continued to stall. "You play tennis?"

"No. Someone just gave me the ball."

"I bet I'd be good at tennis. Man, I'd like to smack this with a racket."

"Let's not waste anymore time."

Mark frowned and returned the tennis ball to the basket.

"I want to revisit a couple of things," the case manager said. "Two of them in particular."

"Shoot."

"Funny you should use that word." The case manager gave Mark an amused look. "One of them was about your alcohol consumption and the other was regarding firearms."

Mark knew he'd eventually want to dig into the details. *Just like boot camp, someone always prying or preaching.*

"You told me before about someone showing you a gun." The case manager scratched his beard. "Tell me more about that."

"A gun?" Mark looked at the wall. "Oh, I know all about guns. Pappy had a whole collection."

"Growing up, there were guns in your house?"

"Sure. Still are. Although most of 'em got sold off after he died. Granny kept the pistol."

"Then just tell me about the pistol."

"What do you want to know?"

"Whatever comes to mind."

"Let me think—" Mark took a few seconds. "When I was about six years old, when I first spent the night with Granny. That was the first time I ever saw it."

"Okay. Go ahead."

"Pappy was away and my mom dropped me off to stay with Granny." Mark recited the same story in the circle at boot camp. "It was a Friday night."

"Okay."

"So when it came time for bed, Granny said I was to sleep in her room." Mark slumped in the chair and let his head drop on the backrest. "She had a big bed and all. So, as I pulled the blankets up, I see Granny come into the room with her hair all tied up and some kind of cream on her face. But then, I noticed something shiny in her hand. It was a pistol.

"She said, 'Pappy told me to keep this near—' and she laid it on the nightstand. She said something like, 'just in case if I ever needed protection.' I looked over and noticed the gun with some kind of lock on the trigger, but it was the real thing. She said, 'Don't you worry about a thing,' and she turned off the table lamp.

"Man, I remember just laying there wondering what exactly it was we needed protection from." Mark looked over at the case manager. "You getting this?"

"I'm listening," he said, scribbling on a pad. "Don't worry about me making the occasional note. You should be used to that by now. Please, continue."

"Well, I laid real still with my eyes shut figuring Granny would think I was asleep. It didn't take long for her. I could tell because she started snoring. Not loud snoring like the *Three Stooges*, but quiet snoring, like a granny. Anyway, all I could think about was why we needed that pistol.

"So, I eased my eyes open. I couldn't see a thing. There was a little bit of light coming through a window. I looked over and could see the pistol. I figured if we needed it, I could hop over Granny and have it in my hands just like that." Mark snapped his fingers. "I focused on that window started thinking how a prowler might climb through it. If I was a prowler, that's how I'd come in.

"So, I watched and waited. Away from the window, I heard the floorboards screech and jerked my head towards the door. I started worrying about someone coming through there. So then, I began to glance back and forth from the window to the door. It was so dark that it really didn't matter. I couldn't see nothing anyway."

"The gun made you nervous?"

"Heck no." Mark glared across the desk. "I was worried about a prowler. We needed the pistol. Pappy wanted us to have it. The whole time I was thinking, 'Don't you worry Granny, I'll stay awake. You just be ready with the pistol if I poke you.' I wanted her to be safe."

The case manager made another note on his pad.

"Whenever I heard another creak, my heart would beat faster. I thought, 'It must be a prowler.' The wind caused a branch to tap against the window and I thought it was someone prying at the lock with a screwdriver. The floorboards would pop and I feared the burglars had tunneled their way under the house. It went on like that all night.

"I started to pray for daylight. I laid under them covers hoping that any minute the window would start getting some light in it. If only daybreak came I'd be able to see. We'd be all right. I kept looking over at that window, hoping it was getting lighter." Mark checked to see if the case manager was paying attention.

"Go ahead."

"So when it finally started to get light, I started to feel some relief. I could make out the things in the room—the dresser, pictures on the wall, the rug. It must've been another hour that I laid there waiting for Granny to wake up.

"When she finally started to stir, I closed my eyes and acted like I was asleep. When she sat up, I opened my eyes. 'Did you sleep well?' she asked me.

"My eyelids were heavy and my eyeballs were dry and I said, 'uh-hum.' I didn't want her to know that I had stayed up all night worrying about a prowler."

"But you weren't afraid because of the gun?"

"That's right."

"Let's take a break," the case manager said. "How about a soda pop?"

"Sure."

They both went to a vending machine down the hall, dropped coins in the slot, made a selection, and pulled cans from the bin. Mark popped the top while walking back to the office. He sat back in front of the desk.

"I think we're making some real progress here," Mr. Shannon said. "Can we continue?"

"Sure."

"Let's talk some more about your experience with alcohol."

Mark wanted to smile, but he knew from experience to remain serious. Having already presented it to numerous counselors, the story was well-rehearsed. "Well, the first time I ever drank a beer, I was twelve years old. You see, a buddy of mine snuck a few cans from his refrigerator. I think I told you about Skeeter before. Well, you see, I think they went through so many beers in that house they couldn't keep count. He hid them out back. We both drank one apiece one night. It was kind of funny and all. It made me a little dizzy, but I wasn't drunk or nothing." Mark stopped and looked over at the case manager.

"That's it?"

"That was the first time. You see, there was a couple more times like that. Then there was the worse time."

"The worse time?"

"Yeah."

"Tell me about that."

"Moose got it started. I think he was old enough to drink, or at least, he never had trouble getting the booze. So they called me over. It was a Friday night. I think they already had quite a few because they were kind of nice to me. They were saying, 'Hey Crowbar, come on and have a beer with us.'

"So up the porch I went. They threw me a can of beer and I popped it open.

"'Chug it!' they both said.

"Right there, next to the 'Cage of Bravery', I felt like it was my duty to show them I could—so I chugged it. I burped real loud, and said, 'Give me another one.'

"They were both howling laughing.

"Well this went on for some time until they went for the whiskey. I remember it was dark outside. We started taking drinks right from the bottle. They passed it to me. The whiskey burned my throat as bubbles rose to the bottom of the upturned bottle. When I tried to walk down the steps, I remember tripping. I fell flat on my face in their front yard.

"They both laughed so hard. I realized that I was face down, right in the middle of the 'Cage of Bravery'. I tried to get up, but had a hard time walking.

"One of them said, 'Hey man, you know what we ought to do?'

"And the last thing I remember, we was walking through the backyard and onto the golf course."

WEEK ELEVEN

Mark arrived at the golf course earlier than usual. He didn't expect Vic for another twenty minutes, so he went inside for a soda. When he returned outside to the practice putting green, alarms were going off in his head. He started to panic. "What happened to my clubs?" He stomped around talking to himself. "They were laying right here."

He scoured the area looking for suspicious characters, and then approached two men sitting in a golf cart. "You guys see a set of golf clubs around here?"

The man in the passenger seat put on a smart look. "There's all kinds of golf clubs around here." He laughed.

"No, man." Mark's voice grew louder. "My golf clubs. I sat them right over there, near the green, and they're missing."

"Hadn't seen 'em son," the other guy said as he stepped out of the cart and walked towards the parking lot.

Mark continued to scan the grounds. He saw Luke Dengel. Mark puffed out his chest. "Was it you?" He could hardly spit out the words. "Did you take my clubs?"

"What clubs?" Luke Dengel looked surprised.

"My golf clubs. Hey man, you know which ones they are. You took them to get back at me—right?"

"I don't know what you're talking about." Luke Dengel held up both hands. "And you better watch where you're pointing. You ever heard about where the rest of them fingers are pointing back to?"

"You've been on my case and now you've stole my clubs." Mark could feel the steam building in his brain. "I'm supposed to be staying out of trouble, but when I find the person that stole my clubs, man, I'm punching their lights out."

"Look, first off, if I were going to steal anyone's golf clubs, your bag wouldn't even make the list." Luke Dengel spit a stream of tobacco juice. "And second, I've been working here six days a week for the past fifteen years. You think all of the sudden I've turned into some kind of golf club thief?"

Mark acted like he hadn't heard a word. "I'm calling the police."

"Have you talked to Shorty or the guys in the cart barn?"

"No." Mark took a deep breath. "Nobody better be pulling any pranks on me."

"Why don't you check around before you get yourself in such a lather?"

Old Georgie walked up. "Those your clubs over there?" he said, pointing to a bag leaning against the side of the building.

Mark tried to dial down the anger. "That's them." He wasn't sure if he should be glad to see them, or remain mad at whoever was playing a joke.

"They were lying right next to the practice putting green," Old Georgie said. "I was on the mower ready to cut the fringe when I saw 'em. I'm sure you wouldn't want me to run 'em over. Where were you? I had to get off the mower and move 'em myself. You should pay closer attention to where you leave 'em."

"Whatever." Mark grabbed the bag and headed for the patio. He sat on the bench and simmered. *I hope they all got a good laugh.*

Five minutes later, Vic strolled up with the cane in front tapping at the ground.

"Hey Vic," Mark said.

"Sorry I'm running a little late," Vic said, folding the cane. "My wife just dropped me off."

"No problem." Mark stood.

Vic said, "You brought your clubs today?"

"Yeah, and would you believe me if I told you I've already had to deal with some hassles."

"What happened?"

"Never mind, let's just get going."

"I don't mind pulling my own clubs around," Vic said, twisting his torso to loosen tight muscles. "Set the bag in a pull cart for me."

"Nah. I'll carry 'em for you. After all, it's part of what I'm supposed to do."

"Suit yourself."

After thirty minutes, Mark figured out that carrying two bags wasn't much fun. Traveling back and forth on the fairway after taking his own shot, then running over to line up Vic had tripled the distance he had to cover. Not to mention, it was very time-consuming. "Maybe this wasn't such a good idea."

"Hey—" Vic shrugged and smiled. "We gave it a try and it didn't work out. At least we learned something."

"Okay." Mark decided to abandon playing his own ball and concentrated on helping Vic. He stood behind and watched as Vic bent over and combed his fingers through the tall grass.

"You're in the rough."

"Just making sure," Vic said. "I didn't think I was in the fairway. Most of the times I can feel it with my feet." Vic took a swing. His club dug into the earth about an inch behind the ball. "*Che stronzo!*"

The double load caused Mark to gasp for air. "You shouldn't get so mad Vic."

"I know kid." Vic relaxed his clenched teeth. "Sometimes I should set a better example."

"You always fake me out when you pretend to break that club over your knee."

"I know." Vic smiled.

"Didn't you tell me it was some kind of rare collectible club worth a bunch of money?"

"Listen kid, nothing's worth nothing until somebody actually pays something for it."

"At least you don't throw it. I've seen plenty of people humming clubs through the air when they get mad."

"Yeah, I should do better. Promise me this—let me know if I ever distract other golfers and need to apologize. It's one thing to be an *idiota,* and quite another to be an *idiota* and not apologize for it."

Mark scratched his head. "Okay."

As they stood in the next fairway, Vic turned in Mark's direction. "What ever happened with the *ragazza*? You know, the girl you told me about? What was her name? The one you had a date with?"

"Linda?"

"Yeah, Linda."

"I see her sometimes. We don't have any classes this year."

"So the old flame's been doused?"

"I guess. She doesn't seem to be so friendly."

"Something you did?"

"I don't know. Anyway, I didn't do anything she thinks I did. I told you she was back with her old boyfriend?"

"You told me."

"It was kind of weird. A couple a weeks ago she passed me in the hallway and gives me this dirty look. I asked her what was the matter and she says, 'I know it was you that farmed my yard.'"

"What does that mean, 'farmed' her yard?"

"You know, when someone drives a car across a lawn. It usually leaves ruts in the grass like a plow going through the field."

"Sounds *sciocco.*"

Mark raised an eyebrow. "So I said to her, 'I don't know what you're talking about. It wasn't me that farmed your yard.' But she just shook her head and said, 'I know it was you.' I could've told her this story of why it wasn't me, but I just got mad because she didn't believe me."

"What's the story?"

"You want to hear it?"

"I'm asking ain't I?"

"My sister, when she was in high school, she had a few crazy boyfriends. There was this one guy that got real nasty when they broke up. Every Friday night, like clockwork, he'd farm our front yard. We could hear him tearing through the yard with the engine roaring and the tires spinning. I have to admit, it was a little scary. Each week, he'd get closer and closer to the house, and I never knew if he would wind up driving through the front wall. So that's why I would never do that to someone else."

"You didn't tell her that?"

"No." Mark shook his head and looked to the ground. "Like I said, she should've believed me."

"Maybe you'll get another chance?"

"Maybe." Mark raised a finger. "But here's the good part of my story. You know, my sister's old boyfriend. I got even with him."

"You confronted him?"

"Not exactly. I was just a little kid, you see." Mark smiled. "But that didn't stop me. This one Friday night, I set a trap. Stacked behind my neighbor's house were these long strips of molding with nails sticking out. They had just got some new carpeting. So, I borrowed those strips and crisscrossed 'em across my front yard. I made sure each one of those nails was sticking up. And man, wouldn't you know it, the dude came tearing across the lawn that night. I was still a little scared, but I had to smile when I heard him tearing across our lawn."

"What then?"

"I laid there in bed not sure if it worked or not. The next morning I went out and looked at the ruts in the yard and knew he had to drive right over the nails. I picked up the strips and put them back in our neighbor's garbage pile. A few days later, my sister learned from somebody at school that her old boyfriend had to go out and buy four new tires. It was the last time we ever heard from him."

"Must feel pretty good to solve a problem like that."

"I have to admit—it did."

"You should've told that to Linda."

"Like I said, she should've just believed me."

As they walked the fairway on the final hole, Vic paused and said, "All this talk about girlfriends has got me remembering back when I was young."

"You got about a hundred yards to the pin," Mark said.

"Anybody behind us?"

"I think we're the only ones out here."

"Good." Vic nodded and pursed his lips. "I guess I can take my time."

Mark placed the clubhead behind the ball. "A little more to the left." He stepped behind Vic. "That's good."

Vic took his swing and made solid contact. "That felt good."

"It turned out good. You're right in front of the green."

As they walked, Vic said, "Like I was saying, it reminds me of when I first met Angela."

"Your wife?"

"Yep. Want to know how I knew she was the one for me?"

"You're going to tell me anyway, right?"

Vic smiled. "We were both just out of college. We went to the same school, but didn't really know each other." Vic took off his hat and ran his fingers through his hair. "But the first time we officially met was at a house party. I saw her across the room and finally said, 'I know you from somewhere.'"

"We spent the rest of that night smiling at each other and recalling all the possible places our paths probably crossed. At the end of the night, just before she left with a group of her girlfriends, she said, 'You should come down to Fitzpatrick's sometime and sit out on the patio with us.' Fitzpatrick's was this local watering hole that had a big wooden deck. It was good for hanging out, eating cheap food, drinking buckets of beer, listening to music, and watching people walk by. So I said to her, 'When?' She said, 'We usually hang out there every Friday.' So I told her that maybe I'd see her there sometime."

"That's it?"

"No." Vic turned his head. "Of course not. That's just the beginning. Here's the thing, I spent that whole week thinking about her. So, when the next Friday rolled around, I said to a couple of my buddies, 'Hey, before we go to the concert, let's stop by Fitzpatrick's.'"

"Was the *strunze* one of your buddies?"

"Yeah, he was there."

"And you were going to a concert?"

"That's a big part of the story. It's like this—I was, and still am, this big Van Morrison fan. And if you know anything about Van Morrison, he doesn't play too many concerts. He's one of those musicians best known for his work in the studio. He's real meticulous about everything. He's not known for great live shows. But sometimes, when he's in a good mood and the stars align perfectly, he is known for remarkable performances. Anyway, like I was saying, I was a huge fan and had pretty good seats to the show. I'd never seen Van Morrison before and had literally waited my whole life for the opportunity."

"He the one that sings that *Brown Eyed Girl* song?"

"That's him, and that's not even close to being his best song. Anyway, so, me and my buddies stop off at Fitzpatrick's before the show. We order a bucket of beers, have a seat, and wouldn't you know it, Angela and her friends come walking up.

"It took my breath away when I saw her again. I had thought about her all week, and when I saw her, she was even prettier than I remembered."

Mark was half-listening. "So that's the story?"

"No," Vic said. "Don't be a *rompiscatole*."

"You gonna tell me what that means?"

"I think you can guess." Vic nodded then turned his face towards the sun. "Anyway, I asked Angela and her friends to sit with us, and after a bucket of beers my buddies were ready to go. I looked at Angela, and I knew right then that I didn't want to leave. I was captivated by her smile. I gave my concert ticket to one of her friends."

"You what?"

"I gave up seeing 'Van the Man' in concert."

"Wait. You said you waited your whole life to go to this concert."

"That's right."

"And you gave it up that easily?"

"Sounds crazy, but yeah. I spent the rest of that night on a patio talking with Angela. We went out on a real date the next weekend, and have been together ever since."

"Is that the end of the story?"

"That's it." Vic smiled. "I found out that sometimes it's good to give up a little to gain a whole lot."

"That doesn't make sense?"

"It will to you some day." Vic continued smiling. "Maybe. Anyway, I never got to see Van Morrison in concert. The next day, my buddies said I missed an epic concert. 'Van the Man' was in a good mood and mesmerized the crowd with one of his best shows ever." Vic turned again to face the sun. "To this day, I still don't feel like I missed a thing."

Mark gazed through the grimy pane and noticed metal mesh bolted to the concrete. He assumed it was there to keep intruders out, but frowned at the thought that it was intended to keep him and his schoolmates inside. He withered in a chair, and remained quiet. *I can't believe they've drug me in here again.* With his arms crossed over his chest, he glanced across the executive desk. There, the principal quietly rifled through an open file.

Mark's sister appeared in the open doorway. "What's this all about?" Her baggy sweatshirt sleeves were rolled up and her hair was in a disorderly state.

Things just got worse.

"According to our paperwork," the school principal began, "you are the legal guardian." He wasn't the same cheery person that greeted his prized pupils in the hallways or addressed the student body during assemblies. When plugged into his desk, only his torso was visible. He was part of the fixtures, a cyborg; half man, half desk. A distorted reflection of the hanging strip lighting appeared in both of his eyeglass lenses and his voice was calm as a robot's.

"You need to change your paperwork," Mark's sister said, pointing with the car keys in her hand. "Mark hasn't lived with us for a while." When she stooped to sit, the purse strap on her shoulder slid off. "He lives with his grandmother."

"I see." The principal scanned through the open folder but wrote nothing down.

"I drove all the way from Spring Hill," she said, stuffing the keys in her handbag and zipping it closed.

"I understand," the principal said. "I'm glad you made the trip. I'm hopeful we can resolve this situation." He rotated his head. "Now that everyone is here, Arthur, will you please tell us again what happened."

Across the room, Art Dimini sat between his parents. His posture was so perfect casual observers would swear there was a board strapped to his back. Art was vying for valedictorian. Since the race was based on grade-point average, he had a chance. The list of his extracurricular activities was longer than his list of friends. He was a member of the Debate Team, the Chess Club, the Chemistry Club, the Glee Club, the Thespian Club, the Photography Club, and he was Editor of Hickory Leaves, which was the yearbook.

Art Dimini sniffled as he raised his head. "Well, like I stated earlier, I was walking through the courtyard and was accosted by him." He pointed at Mark.

"That's a lie," Mark said, shifting higher in his seat. "Definitely not true, man." Mark was the opposite of Art in every way. His lone claim for a class superlative, having acquired more hours than anyone, would be President of the Detention Club; if there was such a thing.

"Just hold on," the principal said, shooting his eyes at Mark as if they were laser beams. "Everyone here will get a chance." He turned back to Art. "I will need details. Please be specific."

"Okay," Art said, stretching his neck like a giraffe. "I was walking from the photography lab towards my locker. I was on my way there to drop off my work before going to the cafeteria. It's the same route I take everyday."

"That's the details we're looking for," said the principal.

"And everyday," Art said, "I have to pass by the crowd of those people smoking cigarettes in the courtyard. Every time I pass by, someone calls out, 'Hey Arty Farty' or 'Hey Arty Farty where's the party?' I can't go by there without hearing some kind of remark like that. Each time I just try to ignore them and walk faster."

"Go on."

"Well, today, I tried to ignore them. 'Why you in such a hurry Arty Farty?' I heard one of them say. 'What's in your purse Arty Farty?' I heard another one of them say. And right after that, my camera bag went flying off my shoulder. When it hit the ground, the camera flew out and shattered to pieces." Art's voice got shaky and his eyes started to water. "That's a four-hundred-dollar camera."

The principal processed the story while remaining unemotional. "And how is Mark involved?"

"Well, when I turned around, I saw him laughing," Art said, regaining some composure. "There were two others around him. They were both looking in different directions and not laughing. I was so mad. I said, 'Who is going to pay for the camera?' And I told them I was going to the principal. But he," Art pointed in Mark's direction, "just kept on laughing."

"Hey Arty," Mark sneered. "You left out the part where you called me an immature *freak.*"

"That'll be enough," the principal said.

Mark continued as if he didn't hear the warning. "Hey man, how many times did I say they were just kidding you?" He produced a sarcastic laugh. "Geez, can't you take a joke?"

"You can say it a million times—" Art crossed his arms in front of him. "But it wouldn't mean a thing. I want to know who's going to pay for the camera?"

"Okay Mr. Crowe," the principal said. "That's enough of that. Let's hear your side of the story."

"First off, like I've said from the start, I don't know nothing about any name-calling or camera breaking." Mark rested his ankle on the opposite knee and began to wag his foot. "Sure, I was laughing, but that was because someone had just told me a joke. Arty started going *berserk* and I didn't even know why. His face was all red, and he was the one going around calling everybody names. Like I've said a million times man, I had nothing to do with this."

The principal formed a steeple with his fingers and began tapping his lips. "And you didn't see how the camera bag happened to leave his shoulder?"

"Like I said a million times—" Mark looked at the door. "I didn't see nothing man."

"You will refer to me as Mr. Sparks," the principal said. "One more MAN will earn you time in detention."

Mark nodded and smirked. *Mister Narks.*

Art's father spoke up. "It is an expensive camera, and it does seem to be damaged beyond repair." He held up the broken camera for all to see.

Mark's sister squirmed a little. Her body language and expression shouted that she would rather be anywhere else.

"Well—" the principal said. "Are these *all* the facts in the matter?"

There was a knock on the glass panel of the door. "Yes," the principal said, "come in."

"There's another student out here," the secretary said, twirling a ballpoint pen. "He wants to see you about the camera."

"I'll be right there." The principal pulled himself away from the desk. "Will you all excuse me please?"

Mark sat next to his sister in silence and watched as Art whispered back and forth with his parents.

Mark's sister whispered, "When are you going to grow up?"

"It wasn't me," Mark whispered back. "And I told them not to call you."

The door opened and the principal reinserted himself behind the desk. "Looks like someone else's guilty conscience has been working overtime." He frowned at Mark. "Another student has come forward and admitted to *accidentally* bumping into the camera."

"I told you it wasn't me," Mark said, smiling.

"Well, I think it's clear to most of us here," said the principal, nodding. "You aren't exactly as innocent as you make out. But, since someone else has stepped up, I'll allow you a pass on this one. You are free to go."

Mark and his sister stood.

"Oh," the principal said. "Before you leave, we'll need to know who to contact as the guardian."

Mark's sister said, "Can we talk about that at a later time? I have to be across town to pick up my kids from school."

"Yes, please notify the office so we can get our records straight. Whoever the contact is, we need to discuss an attendance record that is teetering on the brink."

"Come on," she said, shaking her head. "I'll give you a ride home."

Most of the ride was quiet, but Mark expected a lecture.

"You know," his sister said as they neared Granny's house, "you're going to have to grow up."

"Man, I knew it was coming," Mark said, turning to glare at her. "You couldn't let this slide without a sermon."

"Don't you realize you've ruined my day?"

"I didn't realize you were so busy." Mark looked out the passenger side window. "Besides, it wasn't me that called you," he said in a low voice.

"I meant what I said. I'm not the person to be called for you anymore. I got my own boys to worry about. When are you going to realize you're on your own?"

"I got Granny."

"Granny's too old and you know it. No way could she have made it to school for this. And all your trouble before, you think Granny would have been able to help you through all that? You don't even realize how much Tom and I did for you."

"I knew you would get around to him too—another lecture about you and Saint Tommyboy."

"I've told you before, don't call him that!"

"Blah, blah."

"When are you going to realize the messes you make are yours to handle. The quicker you learn that, the better off you'll be."

"You're sounding like Tommyboy."

"Don't call him that."

"Big deal." Mark stared out the window. "Anyway," he said. "I've got a plan now. I'm getting serious about all this. Once I make it to eighteen, I won't have to worry about anything. And just for the record, I didn't get in any trouble today."

"See, you don't even realize the trouble you caused me. You think you're off scot-free, but my afternoon is ruined. Ever consider that?"

"You're not so busy."

"How would you know? And as for your birthday, I think you're going to find out that once the law considers you an adult, everything changes. You're about to run out of all your second chances."

As they approached the driveway, Mark continued looking out the car window.

They stopped, and his sister said, "You even listening?"

"Yeah man, I'm listening," he said without looking at her. "You coming in to see Granny?"

"I can't. I'm already late."

Mark opened the car door and stood. "Well, tell the boys I said hey."

"I will. And Mark," she said before he could close the door, "I'm serious about all this. You're on your own. Grow up!"

WEEK THIRTEEN

Many times when Mark thought he was heading for the mountaintop, he wound up in a valley. Just thinking about it put him in a sour mood. *Let's get on with this so I can go home.* He acted like he hadn't heard anything. "What's that?"

"I noticed something about you." Vic stood in the middle of the fairway facing nothing in particular. "You don't laugh all that much." The bucket hat kept the sun's rays from burning his scalp and the dark shades covered his eyes. "Why so gloomy?"

"I do a lot of laughing Vic," Mark said, aiming for sarcasm. "If you could see me, you'd know that I'm smiling right now."

"No offense kid, but I find that hard to believe." Vic turned towards his next shot. After Mark lined him up, Vic sent the ball down the fairway. As they walked, Vic said, "You got your whole life ahead of you." He synchronized hand movements with his words. "You should laugh more."

Mark took a deep draw on a cigarette and blew out the smoke. "Oh, I do a lot of laughing."

Vic continued as if he hadn't heard him. "I figured out a long time ago that going through life with a grumpy attitude was no good for anybody. It made me and everyone around me miserable. Know what I mean?"

"Uh-huh."

"Then one day, I decided to change." Vic pointed a finger in the air. "I realized that every single person that walks the earth, if they look hard enough, can find something that offends them. It seems to me some people do that—they wake up looking for something to irritate them. They complain how the world is stacked against them. So, one day, I decided I didn't want to be like that." Vic smiled. "I wanted to be the kind of person that wakes up every morning and finds something good about the world. It's that easy. Everyone has that power. Once you figure that out, it's easy to change how you think and feel."

That's the dumbest thing I ever heard. Mark flipped the cigarette butt to the ground. *Everybody gets mad about something.*

That's what he started to say. Instead, he said, "Where did all that come from?"

"I don't know. Just felt like saying it." Vic turned away. "In case any of it ever makes sense to you."

"You could be a case manager."

"Your attitude is everything."

"I've heard plenty of that before."

"Maybe so." Vic shrugged. "Let me try something different. Let's say you walk into a crowded room of strangers—" Vic scratched his scalp through the hat. "Better yet, let's say you're in a lifeboat after abandoning ship. Do you want to be sitting next to the guy that's complaining and crying about how you're all doomed and that everyone is going to starve to death, drown, or be eaten by sharks? Or, would you look to the guy that is positive and remains calm and starts looking for ways to be rescued?"

"That's an easy one."

"Well, all I'm saying is think about that the next time you get to feeling negative. Decide to stay positive. You might be surprised with the results. Know what I mean?"

"I guess so."

As they waited on the next tee, Vic said, "You know, if something's eating you, I'm a good listener."

"You know Vic, you're about the opposite of Granny." Mark placed his hand on Vic's shoulder. "She can see just fine, but she never picks up on much. It's like you can actually see through them dark glasses."

Vic shrugged his shoulders. "So, what's going on?"

"Well, I've had a bad week." Mark took a few seconds. "That's all."

"Go ahead." Vic nodded. "Get it off your chest."

"Monday," Mark said. "I got caught looking over at someone else's answers on a test. The teacher saw it, grabbed my sheet, and made me leave the room."

"After all the talk about honesty?"

"What talk?"

"Keeping an honest score. Following the rules. Any of that sinking in?"

"I thought that was for golf."

"You some kind of *mamaluk?*"

"A what?"

"*Mamaluk*, it's sort of an Italian phrase. Anyway, things you learn out here apply everywhere. What about your timeline and all. You even trying?"

"Of course I am." He threw Vic an angry glance. "But man, sometimes I just forget and slip up."

"You get a little *stunad?*"

"I guess. Anyway, I begged the teacher to let me take the test over, and somehow I got lucky enough to get another chance."

"Did you pass?"

"I asked the teacher when I finished. She just looked it over and said, 'We'll see.'"

"Sounds okay to me."

"But that's not the worst it." Mark paused. "Today, I think I topped your buddy the *strunze*."

"How's that?"

"It has to do with Luke Dengel."

"Dengel?"

"Yep."

"What about Dengel?"

"I was trying to do the right thing." Mark hung his head. The long hair covered his face. "That goes to show you I did remember one thing. You know, how you said it was good to do nice things without someone having to ask you."

"And you chose Luke Dengel?"

"Yeah." Mark kicked at the grass. "I didn't really choose him, but the chance kind of popped up."

"Go ahead."

"You know how much he likes his car, you know, the cherry-red Thunderbird? He treats that car just like a baby—always buying little gadgets for it, only driving it when the weather's good. He even parks it away from other cars so no one bumps into it. I even heard someone offered him twenty thousand dollars for it, but he turned them down."

"He does love that car," Vic said. "I think he's told everybody the story of how he fixed it up."

"I got here early today—" Mark said.

"Early bird catches the worm." Vic smiled.

"I caught something all right." Mark looked around. "I walked past the old cherry-red Thunderbird and noticed the back fender was dirty, so I swiped my finger across it. My first thought was to decorate it with a few curse words or even a friendly reminder for him to get it washed, but I thought about it and knew he's the last person I should mess with."

Vic nodded. "Sounds like the right decision."

"But that's not the end of it. You see his car was near the cart barn, and some of the guys were hanging around the door. They must've seen me looking at the fender.

"One of them yells over to me, 'Hey man, you want to get in good with Luke Dengel?'

"At first, I thought about ignoring him.

"Another guy said, 'Luke was trying to get one of us to wash his car. But we all told him we were too busy.'

"'Hey man, why you telling me?' I said.

"Instead of answering, he just kept talking. 'He offered to pay Old Georgie twenty bucks.'

"By this time I was standing right in front of 'em.

"Another guy said, 'You should wash it for him.'

"And they all nodded. I heard someone say, 'He'll probably give *you* that twenty bucks.'

"At first, I didn't even think about the money. I was just thinking that maybe this was a chance to get back on his good side. I thought about it, and told 'em I'd do it.

"One guy went and dragged a hose out, and another guy went inside and fetched a bucket of soapy water and a sponge.

"So I stretched the hose to the parking spot and wetted down the car. They stood there and watched as I dunked the sponge in the bucket and started soaping up the old cherry-red Thunderbird.

"I wasn't even half-way around the back bumper when I heard someone yelling. It was Luke Dengel. He was tearing towards me in the maintenance cart. He hopped out and started getting in my face. 'What in hell are you doing?' He started screaming.

"I dropped the foamy sponge in the bucket. 'I noticed your car was a little dirty' I said, 'and I thought you might like it if I washed it for you.'

"Well you should've seen him, I actually thought he was about to haul off and punch me. I thought his head was going to explode. His face was redder than his car and he started screaming something, but I couldn't make it out because his jaws and lips were clamped down so tight.

"He grabbed the hose and started to rinse off the car. 'Get away,' he yelled. 'And if I ever catch you near it again, you'll be sorry you ever met me.'

"At that point what could I do? I just kind of hung my head and walked away."

Vic rubbed his chin. "Well I guess I should've been a little clearer about my advice."

"I heard one of the guys in the cart barn say, 'We was just yanking your chain, man. Can't you take a joke?'

"But I didn't think it was funny."

"Like I was saying, I should've made it clearer." Vic dropped his head. "When you're going to surprise someone, it's best to know for sure that the surprise is something that they're hoping for or will appreciate. You know what I mean? When it comes to my wife, she's always dropping enough little hints for me."

"I kind of got that."

"You took a chance with Dengel, and it didn't quite work out. I'll talk to him—tell him it was my fault. I'll take some of the blame. He's a reasonable man. I think he'll see you were trying to do good."

"But what if he doesn't?"

"Well, some people are like that. Give him some time, maybe he'll change his mind. Who knows?" Vic shrugged his shoulders. "Maybe this will all seem funny to you someday."

Y ou're late," Mr. Shannon, the case manager said, pointing at his wristwatch. His stoic face matched the unsympathetic tone of his voice.

"C'mon man." Mark breathed heavily. "Only by five minutes." Sweat lingered on his brow.

"I'd say closer to fifteen. Look, missing meetings and being late for meetings throws my whole day out of whack. I have a busy schedule—so don't let it happen again."

"You're sure in a bad mood." Mark dropped into the chair. "Somebody take a leak on your lunch or something?"

"I'm serious." The case manager tilted back in his chair and crossed his arms. "If you're late again, it goes in the folder."

Ooooh, please, not in the folder. Don't make me laugh. Mark kept his thoughts private. He smiled and said, "Hey man, I'm sorry."

"Okay." The case manager propped his elbows on the desk. "Let's talk a bit about your future. Have you thought about a career?"

Mark raised his eyebrows. "Career?"

"Yeah, you know, assuming you make it through high school, what are you going to do afterwards? How are you going to pay the bills? Things like that."

"I plan on living with Granny. She gives me a few dollars here and there. I usually keep the change when I go to the grocery. She pays me to cut the grass."

"That may be fine for now, but you should be thinking about the long term."

"Staying with Granny is the long term. I think she needs me to take care of her and all. But, I have thought about making some extra cash on the side."

"Let's hear about it."

Let's see, what would sound good? He hooked each thumb into the opposing armpit. "I think I want to be a juvenile probation officer."

"You do, hmm… What makes you say that?"

"Well, you know, the way you're helping me out, I'd like to be able to do that. Of course, I'd ask for a better office, but you got to be raking in the dough."

"Not really." Little creases appeared on the side of the case manager's eyes when he smiled. "You should know—the job doesn't come with a large salary. My rewards go beyond what I'm paid. Your choice is interesting, but don't take me for a fool." He nodded and blinked. "I've been doing this a long time."

"No, really, it's true." Mark responded faster than usual. "I'd like to work with the cops, you know, cleaning up the streets of all the delinquents."

"That sounds different from my job."

"Don't you work with the cops to make sure all the degenerates are safely rehabilitated?"

"When it comes to the police department," said the case manager, "I'm not even considered part of their pecking order."

"So you don't work for the cops?"

"No," Mr. Shannon said. "But I do often sympathize with the job they do. They deal with the lowest and worst of our society, and we expect them to keep us safe. It's a tough job. And one bad apple among their ranks does real harm to the public's trust. They all get a good smearing. Everyone expects nothing less than perfect. Problem is, whenever people are involved, there's no such thing as perfect."

"You trying to recruit me to be a cop?"

"Not exactly."

"Good." Mark smiled. "Because I was about to tell you about my real job."

"Go ahead."

"You see, me and some friends are talking about putting together a band. We figured we could get gigs all over town. And, you never know man—we may just hit it big."

"Do you play an instrument?"

"Kinda. You see, I plan on being the drummer. I'm always going around tapping on stuff with my hands like they were bongos. Sometimes I use two pencils."

"Do you have a drum set?"

"Nah."

"Don't they have a marching band at your school? Have you taken band classes?"

"Are you kidding?" Mark curled his lip. "I wouldn't be caught dead with those band geeks."

"At least they have instruments."

"Yeah, well, I figured all we needed is a drummer, a bass, and a guitar player. And if I ain't a good drummer, I could always switch to guitar. We hadn't decided who was going to be the lead singer yet. We'll probably just take turns." Mark cocked his head to one side. "You know, the lead singer gets all the chicks. They'd line up for us at the stage door after each show. Man, I'd almost not even worry about the money as long as we had that long line of chicks."

"That's your plan?"

"Not totally." Mark rubbed both hands together. "You see, if it doesn't work out with the three of us, we might consider adding another guy—maybe a saxophone player. That's when we might have to go to the marching band to find someone. Either that, or I'll learn how to play that myself."

"Here's some career advice I'd give you," Mr. Shannon smiled. "Don't count your chickens before they're hatched."

Mark shrugged his shoulders and pulled a pack of cigarettes from his pocket.

"Uh-hum," the case manager wagged his finger and shook his head.

"Oh yeah," Mark said, stuffing them back into his pocket. "I forgot."

"Since you brought it to my attention, let's talk about the smokes."

Mark shrugged his shoulders. "What about it?" *Here we go again.*

"I'm just curious. How'd you get started?"

"Not really sure." Mark looked up at the ceiling. "I think the first time was back in grade school. This one kid waved a cigarette around on the playground. He asked a few of us if we wanted to smoke it. So, I said I would. One kid took a puff and kept coughing and spitting. When it was my turn, I blew smoke rings like one of those rich guys you see in the movies. I kind of liked it I guess. So, I've been smoking ever since. It kind of relaxes me."

"I think I understand."

"Hey man, that reminds me of another story." *Time for some pity.* "You want to hear it?"

"Sure."

"The playground reminded me."

"Go ahead."

Mark looked over at the diplomas on the wall. "Well you see, on our school playground, we had the regular setup, you know, swing-set, monkey-bars, jungle-gym, seesaws, and this metal merry-go-round. It seems like whenever we played on any of that stuff you had to like run around repeating some song to make it more fun, you know, like, 'It's raining. It's pouring. The old man is snoring.'

"But some kids would make up their own little songs and it was usually to pick on people. You know, kind of like making fun of other kids. Things like, *four-eyes* for the kids wearing glasses and *brace-face* for those with braces.

"Well, nothing got me madder than when they sang those songs about me."

"So you were the target of taunts as well?"

"C'mon man. Isn't that what I just said?" Mark clapped a hand on the desk. "I would get so mad. I chased after everybody. I thought I was fast, but it seems I could never catch any of them."

"Did you wear glasses or have braces?"

"Of course not."

"But they taunted you?"

"Didn't I just say that?" Mark clenched his teeth then let go. "It was some kind of a rhyme, but I cant' remember exactly.

"One thing I do remember, it always included the word *birdie*.

"You see, my old man was never around. I think someone made up a story that he was in jail. Well, I guess everyone believed it, so they would sing songs about him being a *jailbird* and I was going to be a *little jailbird*."

"Hmmm." Mr. Shannon leaned forward. "Schoolboy chants on the playground can be cruel." He nodded. "That would make me angry."

"Of course it would." Mark balled up a fist. "It would make anybody angry—especially if it weren't true. I used to get so mad I wanted to explode.

"I remember a bunch of kids riding around on that merry-go-round. They were all holding on to them metal pipes. Some other kids ran along on the outside pushing it faster. The faster it went, the louder they would chant, 'Birdie, Birdie, Jail Birdie.'

"I remember trying to run across that spinning wheel to get at 'em. The thing was turning so fast, man. It knocked me down and threw me off. I remember landing in the dusty ruts along the side. But they didn't stop. They kept on spinning and chanting."

"You didn't tell any of the teachers?"

"You kidding?" Mark bobbed his head to move the long locks from his face. "Of course not. Telling only make it worse. Everybody knows that song about *tattle-tells*." Mark touched at his cheek. "I even scraped my face." A few seconds elapsed. "But do you think I would tell? Do you think anybody cared?"

"So what did you do?"

"I didn't do nothing." Mark froze in the chair. "I tried to not be the one getting picked on."

"Let's take a break."

"I got something else for you," Mark said.

"What's that?"

"You remember how we used to talk about my 'perfect dad' and all?"

"I recall we've had some discussions along that line."

"Well, I've been doing some more thinking." Mark gripped the padded tops of the armrests and pushed himself higher. "Me and Granny was watching world federation wrestling the other night. You should see Granny getting all excited. She yells at the screen and everything. Well, anyway, I decided that I wanted to change my idea of who would be my perfect dad."

Another stretch of silence lingered before Mr. Shannon broke in. "Go ahead."

"The perfect dad for me would be André the Giant."

"André the Giant?"

"Sure man. You ever heard of him?"

"Well, I can't exactly say that I watch professional wrestling."

"You don't watch wrestling?" Mark tilted back his head and looked down his nose. "And, you've never heard of André the Giant? Well, he is not only the reigning World Champion, but he just may be the biggest, baddest dude on earth. He's over seven foot tall, and about four hundred pounds. Nobody in the world can beat him."

"And he would be your perfect dad?"

"Of course." Mark dropped is head. "Nobody in the world would ever pick on you if André the Giant was your dad."

Nighttime with Granny dragged. Hours passed with only sprinklings of conversation while they stared blankly at the first thing Pappy had bought with his pension check; the television console. Lights were turned off and the volume turned up. They never disputed the schedule. Often, Mark had to be reminded that snacks of any nature were not allowed beyond the kitchen. Despite that, he took roost in the recliner and snuck morsels to his mouth. The glowing screen lit the room while the slits at the back wafted dust particles heated from glowing vacuum tubes. It had a numbing effect.

Mark stopped rocking and looked over at Granny. "That church of yours have preachers on the street?"

"Shhhhhh," she said from the sofa. She liked the parts of the movie when Elvis sang. "Tell me at the next commercial."

A gathering crowd was urging Elvis to sing them a song. He succumbed to the coaxing and began to shake and shimmy his way into their hearts.

Mark liked to skip the singing parts. He rose and searched for a knitted blanket. Finding it, he returned to the nest.

Granny turned to Mark. "Now dear, what were you saying?"

"Yeah." Mark stopped rocking. *She likes these stories so much, it's about time I give her a good one.* "Does your church have preachers on the street?"

The loose plastic grill around the screen shuddered as a kid's voice belted out a jingle. He was wishing he was a wiener.

"What's that dear?"

"When I was walking home today—" Mark looked around the room. "Outside the Five & Dime I saw a crowd gathered around this guy. He was standing on top of a bench screaming at people. He was waving this bible around and pointing and calling people sinners. He was yelling, 'Repent!' and saying stuff like, 'Judgment Day is near!'" Mark unwrapped himself from the blanket. "So, do you know him?"

"Doesn't sound like anyone I know."

"Some people stopped to listen, but I just kept walking."

Granny looked confused. "Some of these street preachers come from out of town—from an entirely different denomination."

"Well, I just kept walking with my head down. But then I started thinking maybe he was screaming at me."

"Why's that dear?"

"Well, first off, if you've got some good news for me, the last thing you want, to do is scream it at me. You start screaming at me, and calling me names, the first thing I'm going to think about is punching you in the nose."

"Oh dear." Granny put a hand over her mouth. "Have you punched someone in the nose?"

"Oh, no. I'm still doing good on my timeline."

"Then shush." Granny held a shaky finger to her pursed lips. "Tell me in a minute."

Elvis had returned. He was learning about an unexpected dilemma confronting the good-hearted people. All would be lost if enough funds could not be raised to pay a debt. A few minutes later, Elvis started a new song. This time it was a sad, slow ballad.

Mark went to the kitchen for potato chips. When he returned, fast food workers behind a counter were singing about having it your way and special orders not upsetting them. He looked over to Granny. "So, like I was saying, something happened on the way home."

"What's that dear?"

"It might take a little longer than the commercial."

"Go ahead dear." Granny looked closer. "Are you eating something?"

"Like I was saying—" Mark wiped some crumbs from his mouth. "I was a little ticked off about how that guy had screamed at me about repenting and all. I wasn't really paying attention to anything. But when I went past the Post Office, I heard a bunch of commotion going on inside. I looked through the glass window and couldn't see anything but people standing in line, so I didn't think anything of it.

"But right then, this huge guy came busting through the double doors. I looked right at him, and noticed he had a purse tucked under his arm. I tell you Granny, he was just like a football player busting through the line of scrimmage. He had that purse tucked under his arm like he was carrying a football."

"Oh my goodness."

On the screen, Elvis rallied the distressed townspeople. He agreed to represent them in a competition in hopes of winning enough prize money to save the day.

Granny turned away from the television, and focused her attention to Mark.

"Yeah, it kind of caught me by surprise," Mark continued, shaking his head. "So, right behind him comes this little old lady. She must have been as old as you. You'd probably even know her if you saw her. Well, she comes running out of the Post Office screaming, 'Stop that man!' and, 'He stole my purse!' But she could barely move fast enough to totter after him more than a few feet.

"I looked around.

"Everyone was just standing and doing nothing.

"There weren't any cops around, and the only other man I saw was too old to do anything." Mark scratched his head. "There was that shouting preacher across the street. He must've seen what was going on, but he didn't do nothing either.

"So I figured it was up to me." Mark pushed in the footrest and stood in front of Granny. "So, I said to the old lady, 'I'll get him ma'am.' She looked all out of breath and half scared out of her wits. I said, 'Don't you worry.'

"So I started running. This guy had a pretty good head start, but I was fast enough to maybe catch him. I yelled, 'Hey man, drop the purse,' but he just kept running. He turned a corner and looked back. Then he pulled over a garbage can on the sidewalk to slow me down, but I just hurdled over it. He ran by the vegetable stand at Newbury's and knocked over a couple of watermelons. I just weaved my way through them. He turned left at the next corner. When he did, I saw this bench at the bus stop. I knew it was my chance to get him.

"So I cut the corner real sharp, hurdled up on that bench, and dove right on top of him. Let me tell you, I swooped down on him just like making a tackle on the football field. I always told everybody I could play football, and this proved it. Once I got him to the ground, he didn't put up much of a fight. I wrestled him a bit and started saying, 'Hey man, give me the purse!'

"There were all these people watching. They had to think I was probably a pretty good wrestler too. If I told them I wasn't on the wrestling team, they'd all say that I should tryout. I think they were even cheering.

"So, anyway, this guy is huffing and puffing, and fumbling around with the purse until he finally decided to give it up." Mark nodded. "He kind of looked scared of me.

"He said, 'Here, man, take it.' When I grabbed the purse from him, he jumped up and kept running. At first, I thought about chasing him down again, and giving him another wrestling lesson, but then I decided to just hold on to the purse and get it back to the nice lady."

"Oh my goodness," Granny covered her mouth.

The competition was intense and the outcome hung on uncertainty. Elvis narrowly escaped a few close calls. Reaching the finish line, he edged out the competition to clinch a victory.

"I looked at the purse and it looked like it hadn't been opened, so when I got back to the lady, I said, 'Here's your purse ma'am, I don't think he got anything.'

"And she just smiled real big. She went on and on about how brave I was, and how I was some kind of hero or something, and how nice of a young man I was, and what kind of great parents I must have, and how I should be on the track team because I was so fast, and stuff like that."

Granny wore a look of admiration.

"Then she said she wanted to offer me a reward." Mark was growing breathless from the long recital. "She started digging in her purse.

"I said, 'No ma'am, I can't take anything from you. I'm just glad to be able to help you out. You probably know my Granny, and if anything like this ever happened to her, I would just hope that someone like me would do the same for her.'

"She still tried to give me a few dollars, but I turned them down.

"Then she said, 'Well you tell your granny she has a real hero for a grandson.'

"And so I said, 'I will.'"

Elvis snapped his fingers and wrapped his arms around the lucky girl. His shoulders shook as he serenaded her with an upbeat tune while the credits rolled.

Finally—" Mark took a deep breath and puffed out his chest. "The big day is here."

"Oh?" Vic said casually. "Today's the day?"

"You know it is."

"I hope you've been practicing."

"C'mon Vic." Mark strutted towards his waiting clubs. "How much practice do I need to play a blind guy?"

"We'll soon find out." Vic smiled. "One thing's for sure—I'm glad I won't be counting on you to be my coach."

"You talked to the assistant pro?"

"Talked to Shorty last week—" Vic nodded. "Then again, this morning. He's got enough time to go three holes. And just so you can't complain, he agreed to provide both of us the same service."

"Three holes?" Mark bobbed and weaved. "That's all?"

"That should be enough." Vic rubbed his chin. "Now, what did we agree? Was it two strokes per hole?"

"Yep."

"Over three holes, that's a total of six strokes."

Mark smiled, "That means I subtract six from my score?"

"That's it. Whoever has the lowest score wins."

"And you're still okay with that?"

"If you're still okay about wearing a blindfold."

"No problem." Mark rubbed his hands together. "Definitely no problem."

"So, you'll get the strokes and the bet is on."

"And what are we playing for?"

"We didn't talk about that did we? Well, better keep it simple. I don't want anybody to think I played my teenage guide for anything more than chicken feed."

"C'mon dude, who says you're going to win?"

"I've got it. Why don't we make the stakes a friendly handshake? Whoever loses has to say to the winner, 'You are a better golfer than me.'"

"That's it?"

"I think that's enough."

"Okay, you're on." Mark knew Vic's game well and was sure he could match up. The extra strokes made it a certainty. "Here he comes."

The assistant pro looked haggard. "You guys ready?"

They both responded. "Sure."

Mark looked over and saw a big grin on Vic's face.

"Well I guess the first thing we have to do is level the playing field," the assistant pro said, looking at Mark. "Turn around." He pulled a red bandana from his back pocket along with two handkerchiefs. He folded the handkerchiefs into small squares. "Here," he said to Mark, "hold these over your eyes."

Mark felt the hard knot at the back of his head as the bandana tightened. The snug patches delivered him to a world of darkness. "Hey man," Mark raised both hands trying to feel the emptiness. "Who turned out the lights?"

"Too tight?" the assistant pro said.

"Nah."

"Give me a second and I'll get a couple of pull carts."

"Hey Vic, you really are better looking when I can't see you."

"You better start worrying about golf."

"No problem."

Mark felt someone grab his hand.

"Here's the handle of your pull cart," the assistant pro said. "Stick out your other hand."

Mark felt the grip-end of a club.

"I'll guide you around with a club," the assistant pro said. "I'll stop if any obstacles are in the way. We ready?"

"Yep," both participants answered.

"Then let's head for the tee. I figured we'd play one, seventeen and eighteen."

Groping for clues, Mark felt lost in the darkness, isolated, and primordial. He wanted to slow the pace, but bravado kept him from asking for mercy. *If I trip and fall, it won't be my fault—the pro's walking too fast.* He fumbled into the unknown slightly afraid.

As they came to a halt, the assistant pro said, "Anyone need to stretch first?"

"I'm ready Shorty," Vic said. "I loosened up earlier."

"Me too," Mark said although he hadn't lifted a club from his bag in weeks.

"I'll flip a tee to see who goes first," said the assistant pro. "Looks like it's you, Vic."

"Wait a minute," said Mark. "How do I know you really flipped a tee?"

"You're a quick learner," the assistant pro said. "Sometimes you have to place your trust in others."

Mark tethered himself to his bag by resting one hand on the rim. "Whatever." *I don't' know if I've learned anything.*

"Okay Vic," the assistant pro said, "you're clear to take a few practice swings if you'd like."

Mark heard a shaft cut through the air several times.

"I'm ready," Vic said.

Mark heard some mumbling in front of him then some steps shuffling along the ground in his direction.

"You're all clear," the assistant pro said.

The shaft sliced through the air again and a crack sounded out.

"Good shot," the assistant pro said.

"Thanks Shorty," Vic said.

"You're up mister blindfold," the assistant pro said. "You want the driver?"

Mark released his clutch on the bag and held out his hand. "Of course." The grip-end of the club hit his palm. He started with baby steps as the assistant pro pulled him towards an unknown destination. When the assistant pro let go, Mark remembered a television program about glider planes. He thought about how they released themselves from the end of a tow rope. He felt the same detachment before a clenching pair of hands turned his shoulders.

"Let me point you in the right direction," the assistant pro said. "Let me clear out so you can take a few practice swings." After a few seconds he said, "Okay, go ahead."

First, Mark searched for some balance. Unsure in the darkness, he dropped the business-end of the club to the ground and flexed his knees. Hoping that he wouldn't topple over, he took a timid backswing matched to a very weak follow-through.

"I'm afraid you won't hit it very far if that's all you've got," said the assistant pro.

"I'm just warming up," Mark said, not too thrilled about being ribbed. He took another swing. This time, he took it back further with a wider shoulder turn. The extra effort knocked him off balance and caused him to take a couple of steps. For all he knew, Mark could be halfway back to Granny's house. "Hey man, am I still aiming in the right direction?" He held out his hands searching for any feedback.

"You are if you want to take another practice swing," said the assistant pro.

"Nah, I'm ready to go."

"If you say so." The assistant pro's voice was near.

Mark became rigid when the hands gripped his shoulders again.

"Step back a little," said the assistant pro. "Okay, that's good. Now drop the club. That's it. All-right, now move a little more here. Good. Now, you're set-up perfect. The ball is sitting on a tee and the clubhead is right behind it."

"If you say so."

"Now let me back out of the way. Wait 'til I tell you I'm clear."

Mark started to bend his knees. The fertilized doubts began to grow in the darkness. *Is the ball really there? Was this all a practical joke? Luke Dengel's probably snickering somewhere. I bet it's one of those exploding golf balls. If only I had a little light.*

"Okay," the assistant pro said, "you're clear."

Mark drew the club back slowly. When he could wind it no tighter, he let loose in a downward motion and added power. The shaft sliced through the air. Mark anticipated the point of contact.

The expected collision was lost in the darkness. The clubhead bottomed out and began to rise unimpeded. *What's happening?* The glider plane went into a tailspin. All the arrows on the dashboard gauges were spinning. Mark thought about dirty laundry twisting and turning inside a washing machine. *Which way is up?* Finally, he was slapped on the side of his face by the loamy earth.

"Whoa there big fella," the assistant pro said. "You okay?"

Mark touched at blades of grass clinging to his cheek. As he brushed them, he felt a hand lift him by the elbow. "What happened?"

"You whiffed," said the assistant pro.

"Whiffed?"

"Yeah, strike one. Not to mention, you may want to limit your tumbling to gymnastics class. You want to try again, or just call the whole thing off?"

Mark's first reaction was to grow angry. "Why you laughing Vic?"

"Like I've told you before, I have a great imagination. And right now, the mental picture I'm looking at is hilarious."

"But you're not showing good etiquette."

"I made myself a special exemption. I wanted you to know how it felt when someone else was laughing. Want to quit?"

Mark wasn't going to give up so easily. "I ain't quitting. I'm getting two strokes a hole, and I still say I can beat you."

"Whatever you say," said the assistant pro. "Let me set you up again."

After being guided into position and lined up accordingly, Mark took another swing. The second time was a little better than the first only for the fact that he didn't fall down.

He still whiffed.

"Strike two," the assistant pro said.

"Set me up again," Mark said.

"You've used both your strokes and haven't even left the tee."

"I hear you," Mark said, "but I'll get the hang of this."

But he never did.

Mark only managed to catch enough of the ball on the third attempt to get it off the tee and took nineteen more to get it down the fairway and into the hole.

"Good thing there's no one else out here," said the assistant pro. "It took us forty-five minutes to play one hole. Vic, you had a six, and Mark, I lost count. I don't see why we should go any further."

"I'm just getting warmed up," Mark said, "and a bet's a bet."

Vic said, "What do you think Shorty?"

"Well, I can't stay out here all afternoon," said the assistant pro. "We'll play one more. Looks like no one's on eighteen, let's play it."

Mark said, "That okay with you Vic?"

"Sure."

"How about this—" Mark said. "We start a new bet and just play the eighteenth?"

"So we're down to a one-hole match?"

"Sure, the first one should count as a warm-up."

"Normally, I wouldn't change a bet of this nature," Vic said. "But what I can gather about my competition, I've got no problem with it."

"I still get the two strokes?"

"Sure. No problem kid."

It took forty minutes to play the eighteenth hole with the same predictable outcome; Vic won the hole by eight strokes.

After his putt went into the hole, Mark could no longer stand the unknown. He reached up and untied the bandana. Light streamed into his eyes. It was like escaping prison. "I'm not too happy about losing," he said, "but I'm sure glad to be able to see again." He saw Vic smiling. "Oh, I didn't mean anything about that Vic."

"I know what you meant. Don't worry about it, kid. I'm glad you got to walk in my shoes for a little while."

Mark said, "Stick out your hand."

Vic complied.

Mark gripped the hand and gave it a hearty shake. "You're a better blind golfer than me."

WEEK SEVENTEEN

When Mark pushed in the back door, he felt something push back. He first thought it was a bag of garbage waiting for him. But when the door slid open further, he saw the sagging hose on Granny's leg.

What in the world?

"Granny?"

There was no response.

Mark struggled through the door and dropped to the floor. "Granny! Granny! Can you hear me?" He shook her shoulders lightly.

Her face had a gray tinge and her lips looked bluish. She did not respond.

Mark sprang to his feet and snatched the phone from the kitchen wall. His hands shook as he dialed the numbers. His palms felt clammy and cold.

"Nine-one-one, what is your emergency?"

"Yes, hello." Mark's voice was high-pitched as he gasped each word out. "My granny's passed out on the floor."

"What is your address?"

Mark fumbled in a fog. *Oh God. Hafta think. Stay calm. THINK!* His head cleared and it came to him. After stuttering out the address, he said, "What do I do?"

"Stay calm," said the voice on the phone. "Is she still breathing?"

"I'm not sure. What do I do?"

"Look for signs."

The curled phone cord was stretched almost straight as Mark knelt next to Granny. *This can't be happening.* "I've got my ear near her mouth. I think I can hear her breathing. And, yes, I can see her chest moving a bit."

"That's good," the voice said. "Now stay on the line with me. Emergency responders are on the way."

"Granny!" Mark gently shook her shoulders again. "Can you hear me?"

This time Granny seemed to mumble. She licked her lips. Within a few seconds, her eyelids flickered open.

Mark could hardly contain his joy. "She's coming to." *Please be okay. Please be okay. Please be okay.*

"Keep her lying down until the paramedics arrive," the phone voice said.

"Granny, can you hear me?"

"Mark?"

"Yes, yes, it's me. Are you all-right?"

"Why sure." Granny had her eyes open but wasn't really there.

"You must've fallen or passed out or something. Stay lying. Help's on the way."

"Oh, I'm okay," she said. Yet her face was still grayish and her lips blue.

"Keep her still," the voice on the phone emphasized.

"Lie still," Mark said. A few nervous minutes passed until he heard a rapping on the front door. "Don't move Granny, I've got to let them in."

Mark directed two paramedics to the kitchen. They started to work on Granny.

One of emergency responders looked up and said, "What happened here?"

"I tried to come in the back door. I had to push hard, to open it a little. Then I found Granny on the floor."

"You don't know how she got there?"

"C'mon man." *If he blames me for this, I'll punch his lights out.* "Of course not!" Mark glared.

"Look buddy, we're just trying to find out all we can." Undaunted, the paramedic attended to Granny. "Does she take any medications?"

Mark tried to calm himself. "They're on the counter." He pointed.

The guy stood, looked at the bottles, and noted each prescription. He wrapped a cuff around Granny's arm, pumped it up, and listened through a stethoscope. "Do you have any pain anywhere?"

Granny looked like she had to think about it, and then shook her head.

The paramedic slowly bent each arm and leg. "Do you have any pain when I move this?"

Each time, Granny shook her head. She appeared to be swimming around in a foggy haze. She said to Mark, "Make sure you tell Pappy to fix that faucet today."

Pappy? Fix a faucet? Mark stood silent and dumbfounded.

As they wheeled in a stretcher, Granny protested. "Oh I feel fine. I don't need to go to the hospital."

"You're doing fine ma'am," the paramedic said. "But we want to make sure it's nothing serious. They'll be able to run some tests on you there—to see if there's anything wrong. If everything looks good, you'll be back here in no time."

Granny didn't seem to agree.

"You need to go Granny," Mark reassured her. "I'll be right there with you."

"Oh honey," Granny said, "your mom called today."

My mom? Mark didn't know how to respond.

"She said to make sure the wedding cake was delivered."

"Wedding cake?"

"Make sure you wear your nice suit."

"But Granny—"

Mark rode in the back of the ambulance and took occasional glances at Granny. Her eyes were open and a plastic mask fed her oxygen. Mark thought about her incoherent babble and wondered what to make of it.

Once they arrived at the hospital, Mark was directed to the waiting room. There, he found a pay phone and called his sister. After he answered her frantic questions, she calmed. She told him Tom could pick up the boys from school, and she would be there within the hour.

As Mark waited for his sister to arrive, his only thoughts were of Granny. He hadn't noticed any recent abnormalities. Maybe she did move a little slower and slept a little bit more than most people, but that's to be expected given her age. She ate like a bird, but that was normal too. Granny didn't get much exercise beyond her work around the house, but it had been that way for years. She had seemed fine. Yet something continued to bother him. For forty-five minutes he searched for more clues and came up with the same repeated answer: *I have no idea.*

Finally, his sister arrived.

"How is she?"

"They got her in a room running tests."

"I knew this was going to happen."

Mark thought the comment came with a tinge of blame. "What?"

"You know, she's not getting any younger."

"Oh—" Mark sank into a plastic chair and crossed his arms. "Everything's going to be okay."

After Mark explained everything, they waited in silence.

"You never call me," Mark's sister said after several minutes passed. "When I heard your voice, I knew it was trouble. You only call me when you need something or when you're in trouble. I never thought about Granny."

"Thanks a lot."

"Look, I'm just nervous."

"How do you think I feel? You should be glad I was there."

"I am."

"Then no lectures, please."

Minutes passed.

"You know," Mark said, squirming a little higher in the chair, "if I think about it, Granny had been acting a little weird lately."

"She has?"

"I told you about the stuff she said today, and how she looked. Well, there was something else I should've mentioned. It happened a few weeks ago."

"What's that?"

"I didn't think much of it at the time, and didn't want to raise a big fuss over something that probably was just nothing."

"What is it?"

"I came home one night after dark and figured Granny was already asleep. When I walked down the hallway, her door swung open and she was holding the pistol. She was pointing it at me. She looked all panicked and was saying, 'Don't come any closer or I'll shoot.' I was shocked. I held up my hands and said, 'Granny, Granny. It's me. It's me, Mark.' The hallway light was on and she should've been able to see me, but it took her a long time to finally figure it out."

"That doesn't sound good."

"You're telling me. So the next day I asked her if I could start keeping the pistol in my room, but she didn't like that idea. I even thought about unloading it. What do you think?"

"That's probably a good idea."

They sat through another stretch of silence.

She suddenly put a hand on his knee. "You know, there're probably many more things we should start thinking about."

Mark shifted higher in his chair. "Like what?"

"This could just be the start of things. She could be in the hospital a long time. Let's hope it's nothing serious."

"Oh she seemed to move everything okay. I watched them check her out before they put her on the stretcher."

"Yeah, but you never know. When you get old, a bad fall and broken bones can bring on the end."

"She'll be fine." Mark told her...and himself.

"I hope so. But we've got to start thinking about these things. What if she's not able to take care of herself anymore? What if she needs a full-time nurse? What if she needs to be in a nursing home?"

Each of the what-ifs hit Mark like a punch in the stomach. "She's gonna be okay I tell you."

"What would happen to her house? Where would you live? How would we pay for a nursing home?"

Mark dropped his head. He couldn't remember the last time he'd cried about anything. *Granny's gotta be okay.* A tear formed in the corner of his eye.

After a long stretch of silence, she patted his knee again. "You know Mark, I'm really glad you were there when Granny needed you."

WEEK EIGHTEEN

Mr. Shannon started the session in his usual calm manner. "How's your grandmother?"

"She's going to be okay," Mark said. "They only kept her one night in the hospital. They ran a bunch of tests. Didn't find anything. We got her home all right. She says she feels fine."

"Your sister was there to help?"

"Yeah." Mark remained in his usual slouched position. "She stayed with us the first night—just in case. But then she had to get back home."

"You don't talk too much about your sister."

"You never ask." Mark propped his elbows on the arms of his chair. His interlocked fingers hovered in front of his mouth. "What do you want to know?"

"Whatever you want to tell me."

"What's there to tell?" Mark shrugged his shoulders. "She's older than me. She married Tommy Corvid and moved out. I lived with them for a while. It's a long story, man."

"We've got plenty of time."

Mark took a deep breath then let it out. "One day my mom told me I was going to my sister's. She dropped me off out on the street. I knocked on the door. My sister was surprised. A few days later, my mom called. She said she was splitting town. I'd have to stay there. My sister cried, but I saw it coming."

"Did you know about your mother's plan?"

"I had my ideas." Mark looked to the floor. "Then it all came true."

"That must've been tough."

"You get used to it." Mark paused a few seconds. "I think that's when I realized I was 'that kid'."

"What do you mean?"

"Ah, nothing." Mark shrugged. "Anyway, a few days later my sister drove me back to where I used to live. The landlord had the place padlocked. Said he was going to keep all the stuff inside

because the rent hadn't been paid. All I had left, man, was what I took
to visit my sister."

"And you stayed there for a while?"

"For a little while—until Tommyboy kicked me out."

"Tommy being your sister's husband?"

"You got it *Einstein*."

"Why would he kick you out?"

"We got along all right at first, but we started to get into more
and more arguments. He was always giving me the old, 'This is my
house, so you'll live by my rules' speech. He treated me like a child.
Always wanted to know where was I going, where I'd be, what was I
doing, what time was I going to be home. Stuff like that."

"Did the arguments ever get physical?"

"Nah, nothing physical. We may have pushed each other
around a little. One time I shoved him in the chest. Another time, he
pushed me in the back. But there was nothing physical."

"I see."

"So everybody agreed that I should go live with Granny for a
while. Pappy had passed away and she was happy to have me."

"This was your sister's idea?"

"I got the feeling she was ready for me to leave." Mark
looked up at the ceiling tiles. "I liked living with them a little while. I
did have fun with the boys while I was there."

"She has children?"

"Yeah, Corey and Terry—they're a riot." Mark smiled. "We
liked watching cartoons."

"You got along with them?"

"Oh yeah." Mark stared at the desktop. "Not so much when
they were babies and cried a lot, but now that they're older, we have
fun. As a matter of fact, if it weren't for me, they both probably
would've burned up in a fire."

Mr. Shannon leaned forward. With his long shirt sleeve, he
dusted off a spot on his desktop calendar. "Burned up in a fire?"

"Both of 'em." Mark nodded. "See, this one Saturday
morning my sister had to run to the store. Tommyboy was working,
so she asked if I could watch the kids. Well, she didn't remember that
she had left a casserole in the oven.

"By the time she got back, the fire trucks were out front with their lights flashing. The kitchen window was busted out. Smoke had turned the kitchen walls black, and the place was soaked from the fireman's hoses.

"Long story short, she blamed me for not catching the fire before it got started. She's the one that left the thing in the oven and she blamed me. Man, she didn't even thank me for saving her kid's lives. I pulled 'em both from the house—one under each arm. I sat 'em down at the mailbox and said, 'Wait here, don't move.'

"I went back inside, and by that time, it was too late. The fire was roaring from the oven and eating up the curtains. I had a hard time seeing through the black smoke and it was choking me to death. I coughed for days after that."

"But everyone was okay?"

"Oh, sure. A neighbor had called the fire department."

"And they got there on time?"

"Soon enough." Mark nodded. "I stood outside next to the boys and we watched them come and spray down the house. Them boys was right by me the whole time. If it weren't for me, they probably would've gotten burned. Little Terry wanted to go back in the house to get his comic books. I said, 'No.' If it weren't for me, he probably would've run back inside."

Mr. Shannon rubbed his beard. "Sounds like you did the right thing."

"That's what I say. But, you think my sister and Tommyboy think that?" Mark turned his head. "No."

"That's some story."

"You're telling me."

Okay—" Mark raised a hand to shade his brow. "You got about 150 yards to the green. Whatta you want?"

Vic nodded. "Give me the 7-iron."

Mark drew the club from the bag and delivered it into Vic's open palm. Mark held onto the shaft as if he were a tugboat tied to a cruise ship, and pulled Vic into a slot adjacent the ball. Mark let go and stepped back. "You're clear."

Vic milked the grip like it was a cow's udder, and then took a few practice swings.

Mark looked around then spat. "You do that same thing every time."

"What's that?"

"Every time before you swing, you bend your knees like you're about to take a seat."

"It helps me get loose." Vic wiggled some more. "Gets me focused. Know what I mean?"

Mark shook his head and wanted to say how goofy it looked. When Vic went into the second part of his customary preparations, Mark could hold his tongue no longer. "And that same little twist you do with your waist and the little circles at the end of the club."

"You mean the waggle?"

"That another *Italian* word?"

"No, that's a *golf* word."

"Whatever." Mark sneered. "Don't you get tired of doing the same thing every time?"

"Golf is all about doing the same thing every time."

"Even if it makes you look goofy?"

"I gave up looking goofy a long time ago." Vic turned and started the routine over. "My little ritual is no different than a baseball player. You ever see a guy step into the batter's box and tap the plate?"

"Sure."

"Some guys even tap their cleats or tighten their batting gloves. Some guys even cross themselves and say a prayer. They do the same thing every at bat. That's all I'm doing." Vic turned in his direction. "It's my way of telling my brain to get ready and get focused—block out everything else because we're about to do something that requires a little concentration. Know what I mean?"

"It still looks goofy."

Vic shrugged his shoulders. "That's not enough to convince me to change. Now, line me up."

"I was just kidding around. Can't you take a joke?" Mark squared the clubface behind the ball then stepped back. "A bit more to the left."

Vic pivoted slightly.

"There."

Vic flexed his knees, wiggled his hips, circled the club, and then made his swing. The blade of his iron clipped the top of the ball. "Agh! *Marone.*"

"What's the matter Vic?"

"I hit that one terrible."

"Yeah, but you ended up okay."

"That was just lucky."

"But it turned out good." Mark nodded. "Doesn't that matter?"

"Not when it comes to golf. You can't count on luck in golf. Luck comes and goes. You know what I mean? If you're counting on it all the time, sooner or later, your luck will run out." Vic pointed the grip-end of the club in Mark's direction. "I'd rather be consistent."

As they walked toward the green, Mark said, "I've got to give you credit. If I were you, I don't think I'd ever bother playing golf."

"You kidding?" Vic stopped walking. "I love it."

"But wouldn't it be better if you could see?"

"That's probably true about a lot of things, but that doesn't stop me." Vic turned his head. "Believe it or not, wanting to watch where the ball goes is a detriment. Good golfers concentrate on making the perfect swing, and that's what I try to do." Vic turned away. "Anyone behind us?"

"No." Mark shook his head. "Not too many people around today."

"Sure, I miss watching the ball." Vic nodded and they progressed towards the green. "Why do you think they're always telling everybody to 'keep your head down'?" Vic gathered his fingertips into his thumb and stirred the air. "It's because we all want to watch the ball fly. Each shot is like a new creation. Anybody that ever created anything loves to sit back and admire it. I do miss that part. But, from the way I make contact, I can pretty much picture the ball in the air and dropping onto the green. Sometimes I can even hear it landing on the soft turf. I can still feel it. And there's nothing like catching one dead solid in the sweet spot."

"I know what you mean."

"It's a great feeling." Vic placed his hand over his heart.

Mark stood behind Vic on the putting green. "Little more to the left."

Vic swiveled.

"That's good."

Vic made a long putting stroke that sent the ball rolling. "And don't go feeling sorry for me. Since I lost my sight, I've tamed that urge to look too soon. I'm at a point now where I'm not sure I'd change things back if I could. I've adapted to this world and find it just as rich."

"Even in golf?"

"Especially in golf. The sounds are clearer. The smells are sweeter. And there's no better excuse to spend time outdoors. Don't you remember what I told you about golf and how it helped me get better after the accident?"

"I don't remember." Mark lowered his head. "Anyway, I'm sure it's good exercise."

Vic made the short putt and they walked together towards the next tee.

"There's something I got to tell you," Mark said.

"Go ahead, kid."

"I'm not trying to make a joke here, but I've been thinking about our match." They reached the tee and halted. "I have to tell you it was a real eye-opener for me. I tried to think of something else to call it, but I can't think of anything better than to call it an EYE-OPENER."

"I know what you mean." Vic half-laughed. "I use the same phrase sometimes."

"But I'm serious. I never tried anything like that. You know, getting around without being able to see."

"It takes some getting use to."

"Most of the time, when I was standing out there waiting, all I was doing was trying to listen."

"I know what you mean."

"It was different." Mark rubbed his jaw line. "I heard your voices, and I could guess about how faraway you were. Then I felt the breezes coming from different directions. The sun was warm on the top of my head and on my arms. I could even smell the grass."

"It was a glimpse into my world." Vic nodded. "Oh, and I guess you know what I mean by that?"

"I do. And, that's kind of funny. But I tell you, I was never so happy as when I got to take off that blindfold. I don't mean to rub it in or anything."

"I understand."

"You mind if I ask you a personal question? And you can say 'no' because you never pry into my business."

"I don't mind." Vic gestured with an inviting wave. "Go right ahead."

"How'd it happen, you going blind and all?"

"I'll spare you all the gory details—" Vic took a deep breath. "It was an accident. It happened when I was working for the power company. I was up in the bucket getting ready to work on a transformer. Sometimes you can take all the precautions in the world, yet the unfortunate occurs. It blew. I lost my sight because of an explosion. It burned my corneas."

"I knew it."

"What'd you know?"

"I heard Old Georgie telling one guy you were a millionaire. He was saying you should be riding around in a limo."

"And you believe that kind of *crappola?*"

"No. I didn't mean it that way."

Silence lingered.

Mark started to feel bad and hoped he hadn't crossed the line. He respected Vic more than anyone else. Mark aimed Vic's club in the right direction for the tee shot then moved away. "You're all clear."

Vic's swing clipped the top of the ball. "Ah *marone*." Vic threw his hands in the air. "Must've 'looked up' on that one. Now, don't that sound funny?"

"I don't see how you do it—just like what you said right there." Mark nodded. "You know, sometimes you get mad, but mostly you're always cracking jokes and in a good mood. I don't see how you do it." Mark grabbed the pull cart handle. He towed the bag on one side and guided Vic on the other.

"I stay positive." The smile returned to Vic's face. "This may sound crazy, but I'm always reminding myself to stay positive. Know what I mean? I even came up with my own saying. Want to hear it?"

"Do I have a choice?"

"No."

"Then let's hear it."

"You know that phrase, *'If life gives you lemons, then make lemonade.'* You ever heard that one before?"

"I think so."

"Well, I think it means, that if life gives you something sour, you should try to turn it around, and make it something sweet, make it bearable so you can drink it down. It's like all your problems can be solved by just adding a little sugar."

"I get it."

"So here's my version," Vic smiled. "What I say is this, *'Life gives you an apple tree.'* The reason I say *apple* tree is because apples come in both sweet and sour flavors. You've heard of sour apple haven't you? So, my point is, life gives you both sweet and sour, both good and bad—like an apple tree. Know what I mean?"

"I get it."

"So I say, *'Life gives you an apple tree, so pick all the apples, squeeze out every last drop, and drink some apple juice everyday.'*"

"I don't get it."

Vic pressed his palms together. "What I'm saying is that everybody gets handed both good and bad, you know, sweet and sour. All I'm saying is accept that fact. Embrace it. Don't ignore it. Deal with it. Do the best with what you get. It happens to everybody. With a little bit of time, you'll realize some of the sour wasn't so sour and some of the sweet wasn't so sweet. Mix 'em together. Learn to like 'em both. Drink it up every day."

"Why not just say all that?"

"It's too long." Vic shrugged. "And probably nobody would ever listen."

"I think I like the lemonade one better."

"What can I say?" Vic shrugged his shoulders. "I'm still working on it."

"One more thing," Mark said, smiling and feeling friendly. "I think I finally figured something out."

"What's that kid?"

"It's about our match." Mark placed a hand on Vic's shoulder. "At the time, I was kind of mad because I thought I had lost. But, I finally realized, I didn't really lose. You just plain beat me. You are better than me."

"It probably wasn't such a fair match to begin with."

"No kidding, you're good." Mark gave two pats on Vic's shoulder. "And no matter how angry you get when you make a bad shot, you're not like your old pal, the *strunze*."

"You might figure out one day how wrong you are about that."

Mark had logged so much time in the passenger seat, he felt like he should be halfway across the country. From the time his sister had picked him up at Granny's, they had driven across town making stops at the library, the bank, and the drugstore. After that, they waited in the carpool lane at school for thirty minutes. He fiddled occasionally with the radio knob searching for different stations to hold the conversation to a minimum.

At one point, his sister said, "I'm glad you decided to visit us."

Mark just nodded.

By the time she pulled into the supermarket, his legs had grown stiff and the upholstery felt like a bed of coals.

"I won't be more than five minutes," his sister said, steering the car into a parking space adjacent to the shopping cart return bin. She looked into the rearview mirror. "Why don't you all just wait here in the car?"

Terry leaned over from the backseat. "Can we listen to the radio?"

She stopped for a second as if to contemplate the request then looked over at Mark. She pulled the keys from the ignition. "No, I might need these with me."

"Tell us a story," said Corey just as the door slammed. "We watched a movie about knights and we want to hear a knight story."

"A night story?" Mark flipped down the visor and looked at him through the vanity mirror. "A story that happens at night?"

"No, no, a story about the knights, you know, from the olden days. The ones that wore armor."

"Oh, a knight story." Mark massaged his scalp. "I'm not sure I know any of them."

"I thought you said you knew everything." Terry smirked.

"Well, I do, but a story like that might take some time."

"You heard how long the grocery list was."

Together, the boys started chanting, "Story. Story. Story." They drummed the tops of the headrests in unison.

"All right, I think I know one. It's about this dude called the Black Knight." Mark turned to face them, leaning his back against the dashboard. "See, there once was this Black Knight. They called him the Black Knight because his suit of armor was black. It was that way because he never washed it, and didn't have anybody to wash it for him. Like silver knives and forks—if you don't wash and polish it, it turns black."

They both nodded.

"Let's see, he had the helmet with a visor with slits that he could drop down. Um, he had the metal chest protector and arm pads. He had metal gloves, and a shield that kind of looked like a garbage can lid. He also had metal pants that protected his legs, and his boots were also covered, in case anyone tried to stomp his toes."

"We know what a Knight looks like," said Corey. "Tell us the story."

"Hold your horses." Mark held up his hands. "This is all part of it. And speaking of horses, the Black Knight had a horse. His name was Harley. And Harley had a metal helmet and shoulder pads too."

Terry said, "What about a sword?"

"Yep, the knight had a couple of swords. One was tucked in his belt. He also carried around this spiky metal bowling ball that was chained to a stick. Man, he had all kind of cool weapons."

"But what did he do?"

"I'm getting to that. See, you got to learn about the knight first. Did you know that to become a knight you had to have no mother or father?"

"But why?"

"Well you see, the head knight, or maybe it was the king. Yeah, it was the king that wanted all the knights to obey only him. He didn't want any of them getting homesick and taking off in the middle of a fight. He also didn't want any knights ripping off his treasures and sending them back home. So the king made a law—all knights had to have no mother or father."

"I never heard of that."

"It's definitely true." Mark nodded and held up a finger. "Look it up. Now, they also had these contests. They practiced for these knight tournaments for a whole year hoping to win a trophy. And if they won a trophy, they could impress all the smoking-hot ballerina babes up in the stands. It would probably even mean that they would be able to marry one."

"Get to the good part," urged Corey.

"So, the Black Knight, see, he used to practice for these tournaments with these two other knights in a castle down the street."

"What were their names?"

"Their names?"

"Yeah."

"Let's see, there was the Gorilla Knight because he was bigger than everybody else, and there was the, um, let me see if I can remember. There was also the Chihuahua Knight."

"What's a Chihuahua?"

"It's a little dog that barks a lot." Mark looked out the window. "Anyway, the Black Knight would get ready for the tournaments by practicing with the Gorilla and the Chihuahua. The Gorilla usually beat them both since he was about two times as big. But sometimes the Gorilla would make the Chihuahua and the Black Knight fight it out against each other in this cage of bravery. He also made them jump off of high stuff and filled their mugs with root beer to see who could drink it the fastest. All this stuff was good training for the tournament."

"It wasn't like that in the movie."

"Because that's different." Mark glared. "I'm telling you now, so listen." He took a deep breath. "The biggest contest was when they would get on their horse wearing all the gear and grab these long poles and go charging at one another. They would hold out that pole and try to knock the other dude off his horse."

"That's called jousting," said Terry.

"Yeah," Mark said. "I know, and that was the biggest game. If you could win that one, you pretty much would win the whole tournament. Man, sometimes these horses were running so fast, and the ends of those poles were so sharp, they would knock off an arm or a leg, or even stab right through a dude—wouldn't matter if they were wearing the armor or not."

"But what about the Black Knight?"

"I'm getting to that. See, the Black Knight went and signed up for one of those tournaments. He and Harley had been training real hard and studying the competition. He was pretty sure he could beat everybody there. He looked up in the stands and had his eye on this one ballerina. He just knew that the trophy would be his, and that that ballerina would be his too.

"But just when the Black Knight was getting on Harley, these judges came over yelling at him telling him he was disqualified.

"The Black Knight asked them why and they said, 'Hey man, you've been seen hanging around the Gorilla Knight and the Chihuahua Knight.'

"And since the Black Knight was a good knight and all, he couldn't tell a lie. He had to admit that he had been practicing with them.

"The judges said, 'Well then, you are disqualified.'

"The Black Knight asked, 'But why?'

"And the judges told him that the Gorilla Knight and the Chihuahua Knight are known cheaters, delinquents, criminals, and offenders against all of society. And that anyone associated with them was automatically disqualified from all knight games."

Terry grimaced. "No fair."

"That's exactly what the Black Knight said."

"Then what?"

"Well, the Black Knight looked at that beautiful ballerina in the stands and knew she'd never be leaving with him. And man, that made him sad. So sad, that he decided to leave town. He thought about giving up on being a knight all together."

"Aw—" Corey slapped the top of the headrest. "That's not a good story."

"Well, listen, I'm not done yet. And neither was the Black Knight. You see, he had one magic trick saved up. It was something that he had learned from this wizard. It was a trick that let him turn himself into any animal he wanted to be.

"So, he decided to turn himself into an eagle. He knew everybody liked eagles—they were painted on a bunch of the grandstands and on the flags around town. And if they didn't like eagles in that town, since he could fly, it would be easy for him to get to the next town. So, he turned himself into an eagle and began to fly around. To this day, he's still flying around hoping to find a place where someone will give him a fair chance."

Mark's sister pushed the shopping cart down the side of the car and opened a back door. "Move over and make room," she said, dropping bags of groceries onto the seat. "I told you it wouldn't take long. I'm sure waiting in the car was more fun than grocery shopping." She plopped into the driver's seat and gripped the wheel.

Corey bounced in the back seat. "Mark told us a story."

"He did?" She looked over at Mark. "Maybe leaving you all in the car wasn't so smart after all?"

He gave her a dirty look.

She said, "Just kidding."

Mark sensed the cramped walls of Mr. Shannon's office closing in. He had felt the squeeze before, but never to this extent. He fidgeted with the nameplate at the front of the desk. "What would happen if I just skipped town?"

"That's an interesting question." Mr. Shannon stroked his beard. "Something bothering you?"

"I don't know."

"We're pretty close to the end. I'd like to think you'd finish."

"What would happen if I didn't?"

"I think we've made enough progress. I'd probably consider that before making any final decision. But you're so close—you should be happy."

"I guess."

"It would be a real feather in your cap."

Mark raised an eyebrow. "But I just don't know how I'm going to manage without you."

"Oh—" Mr. Shannon leaked out a chuckle. "You'll be fine. Not that I won't miss you, but I hope you'll stay out of trouble."

"That's just it." Mark wilted in the chair. "You know, I've done that, but it doesn't feel like much has changed. Even if I make it a few more weeks, I'm not so sure things will be much different. I see that now. I was just hoping man, that it would be a bigger deal and all."

"What kind of bigger deal?"

"I don't know."

"And what would 'skipping town' accomplish?"

"Oh, I don't know. Maybe a change of scenery wouldn't be bad. You know a fresh start—somewhere where I could have a chance."

"You think your troubles have to do with where you live?"

"I don't know."

"Ever had thoughts of 'running away' before?"

"I don't know," Mark looked at the ceiling tiles. "My sister always talks about my first day of school, but I don't remember it much."

"What happened?"

"The story goes that about thirty minutes after I got dropped off, a neighbor saw me walking along a busy street. They said I could've been killed in the rush hour traffic. I said I couldn't find where I was supposed to go, and decided to walk back home. All I remember was trying to get inside the building that morning. Every door I tried was locked."

"So you decided to walk home?"

"That's how the story goes."

"That's interesting."

"Maybe, but that's just it. You see, it's never like that for the 'it' kid."

"What do you mean?"

"It all came to me. You see, I watch a bunch of movies and hear different stories. People are always feeling sorry for the 'it' kid. It's always an orphan or someone that has run away from home or it's some kid dying in the hospital. He's the 'it' kid. That person always gets the special treatment, you know, free tickets to the circus, or a shopping spree. And if he's lying in the hospital—he gets someone to hit a home run for him."

"So, you don't want anyone feeling sorry for you?"

"That's just it, man. I've never been the 'it' kid. No one ever felt sorry for me. Instead, it seemed they all had it in for me."

"That means you want people to feel sorry for you?"

"I never got my free tickets to the circus," Mark looked him in the eyes. "I never got my free shopping spree. Nobody ever hit a home run for me."

"You never got yours?"

"C'mon man, don't you think I'd remember something like that?"

"That's interesting. What about your grandparents? What about your sister?"

"They're different."

After a few seconds, Mr. Shannon said, "How about this? I'd be disappointed if you decided to 'skip town.'" He drew quotation marks in the air.

"Don't worry too much. I haven't made up my mind." Mark slumped back in the chair and grabbed the tennis ball. "Remind me again. Whatever I tell you is top secret. You can't go squealing to the cops."

"You have my word."

It took Mark a few seconds to collect his thoughts and put the story together. "A few days ago—" He cleared his voice. "Something happened."

"Go ahead."

"I was walking past this certain house, and a certain pair of brothers yelled at me, 'Hey Crowbar, come have a beer with us.'

"I was thinking, only a few more weeks to go, just talk, don't drink any beers or anything else.

"So the older brother said, 'Hey Crowbar, we got a deal for you.' And his younger brother was standing next to him echoing everything he said, 'Yeah, a deal for you.'

"The older one looked around. 'You know that Thunderbird that's always parked over at the golf course?'

"I said, 'Yeah man, I know which one you're talking about.'

"And he said, 'We know too.' And the younger brother echoed, 'Yeah, we know.'

"So I started getting a little nervous, I wasn't exactly sure what they had up their sleeves.

"The older one said, 'One day last week, we followed the goober home. We found out he parks it right in his driveway.'

"So I said, 'What do I care?'

"Then the younger brother looked at me and said, 'What do you care?'

"Then the older brother answered for him, 'We've been thinking about changing ownership.'

"I kind of played dumb at this point and said, 'Look man, I know the guy, and I don't think he'd ever sell it.'

"That's when the older brother said, 'We're not talking about buying it.' The younger one said, 'Yeah, not buying it.'

"I knew perfectly well what they were up to, but I didn't say nothing.

"But the older one made it clear. 'We thought about hotwiring it at the golf course, but too many people hang around there. That's why we followed him home. We figured it would be easier to boost it from his driveway. We'd wait until night, when it's dark and nobody's around.'

"The first thing I thought was I didn't want any part of it. I had made it so far without any trouble and didn't want to even know about their plan.

"And that's when I started thinking about skipping town."

Mr. Shannon propped his elbows on the desk. "I see."

"I knew I couldn't act all worried, so I tried to play it cool. I said, 'Hey man, why you telling me this?'

"And he said, 'We want to know if you want in?' The younger brother was getting all excited. He smiled real big and asked, 'You want in?'

"So I kind of kicked at the ground and lit a smoke. I knew no matter what, I wasn't going to *be in on it*. I tried to make it look like I was giving it some thought. I said, 'Why do you need me?'

"That's when the older brother said, 'We need somebody to drive us and be the lookout. We figured it'd be easier and quicker if there were two of us working on the car.'

"I took a big draw on the cigarette and blew out some smoke and asked, 'But why should I, man?'

"The older brother said, 'You sure you don't want a beer?'

"I just shook my head.

"Then he said, 'We trust you. And besides, we know we can sell the car pretty easy. I know this dude that pays cash money. Whatever we get, we'll split it three ways.

"I tried to think of a good excuse, but nothing came to mind. Instead, I just said, 'I'm not sure, man.'

"The older brother said, 'Think about it.' And the younger brother tried to look all serious and said, 'Yeah, think about it.'

"So I've been thinking about it." Mark looked across the desk. "And skipping town might be one way to solve it."

Mr. Shannon tilted back in his chair. Silence lingered until he finally leaned forward again. "That's some story."

"Well, first off, you don't have to worry about telling the cops about anything, because I don't think anything's happened. The only reason I'm telling you is to prove that making it to my birthday hasn't been easy."

"So what are you going to do?"

"Like I said, it hasn't been easy. I've laid awake at night. You know, like I said, no one ever gave me free tickets to the circus or hit a home run for me. Maybe a little extra cash would be like my shopping spree." Mark reached down and retied a loosened lace. "I'm only telling you because it was bothering me."

"So, what are you going to do?"

"I don't' know."

Mark froze in the fairway when he heard the question. He knew Vic couldn't see his reaction, but wondered if he had picked up a hint of unease. Mark acted like he hadn't heard. "What's that?"

This time Vic paused and turned to face him. "I said did you hear about Luke Dengel's car?"

"Luke Dengel's car?" Mark tried to calm his nerves. "What about it?"

Vic bent his knees and went through his pre-shot routine. He made a swing then said, "It was stolen."

"Stolen?" Mark's voice leapt higher.

"Yep, from right in front of his house."

"How'd you know?"

"Everybody in the proshop was talking about it. Luke was cursing up a storm. Shorty was trying to keep him calm."

"I told you how much he liked that car."

"Well, it looks like the old cherry-red Thunderbird is gone forever."

Mark mumbled, "He'll probably blame me."

"What's that?"

"Nothing."

Mark pulled the clubs behind him with one hand and guided Vic towards the green with an extended golf club in the other. "I hope he doesn't blame me."

Vic looked puzzled. "Why would he do that?"

"He likes to blame everything on me."

"If you had nothing to do with it, why worry?"

"That's true." They reached the green and Mark said, "You don't think I had anything to do with it, do you Vic?"

"It was the last thing on my mind. But the more you talk about it—"

"Well, I had nothing to do with it."

"Then I believe you."

Mark lined up Vic on two consecutive putts and they finished the hole. They walked towards the next tee. Mark said, "Even if I had something to do with it, and I'm not saying I do, I'm not sure it would matter all that much."

"Now you're sounding a little *stunad*." Vic came to a halt. "What's eating you?"

"Nothing really." Mark stopped near a drained ball washer. "It's just that I've been doing pretty good staying out of trouble and all, but I'm really not sure if it means much."

Vic released his grip on the club. "I always thought it did."

"I know."

"I figured it out a long time ago." Vic held a finger in the air. "My whole life is nothing more than little timelines. Some of them I make and feel good about it. Some of them I fall a little short and that's okay too—I usually learn something then. It's nice to always be working towards something. It gives you purpose. You thought about what's next for you?"

"Not really."

"What about school?"

"I've been trying. I'm making it to class. I haven't failed any tests in a while."

"There you go."

"But that's just it. It feels like there should be more. I don't think there's any reason behind it."

"Now I'm not sure I understand."

"Well, it's like this. I don't know if it really matters if I stay out of trouble."

"Now I get it." Vic pursed his lips and nodded. "I have to admit—that's the stupidest thing I ever heard."

"I mean it Vic." Mark kicked at the dirt. "And don't take this the wrong way, but I've been thinking about how nice you've treated me and all. And well, sometimes I wonder if you could see what I really looked like, you probably wouldn't have ever given me a chance."

"Don't ever assume you know what I'm thinking kid. Most of the time, you'd probably be wrong. Know what I mean?"

Dangling long hair covered Mark's face. "Too many people just look at me and don't give me a chance."

"You remember when you were telling me about looking at girls, and I told you I could get a better picture of what people look like on the inside?"

"I guess."

"Well it works on everyone." Vic gestured with his hands. "Now listen, you're not perfect. But you have to realize, nobody is. You're not a bad guy. Think about a few things. What about your grandmother?"

"Granny's getting pretty forgetful and we don't talk much. I'm not sure she even knows anything. If I went away, she probably wouldn't remember I ever lived with her."

"Didn't you tell me you're doing more of the cooking and cleaning around the house since she came home from the hospital?"

"I do."

"Didn't you say you was making sure she was taking all her medications?"

"I do."

"So there you go. That's just two little things that makes you more important."

"Maybe."

"You were there when she needed you before. And the things you're doing now, that's something to be proud of."

"Maybe."

"And, what about your sister and her family?"

"Well, they live far away. I never see 'em much. I get tired of the sermons. They never really see any of the good stuff I do. They're probably both just waiting for me to mess up."

"What about your nephews?"

"Maybe they think I'm all right."

"I'm sure they do."

"Maybe."

"And do I have to remind you that you also got me?"

"You?"

"Sure. I care about what happens to you."

"But I thought all this was community service."

"I'll agree that's how we got started. But, the time we've spent together, I have to admit, you've kind of grown on me kid. Know what I mean?"

Mark felt warm inside. He couldn't find the words to respond.

"And here's something else," Vic said. "I think you're a real *bravo ragazzo*."

Mark smiled. "You going to tell me what that means?"

"Someday." Vic smiled. "But I think you get the gist of it. It's like this—I don't think a bad guy would take care of his grandmother like you do. I don't think a bad guy would brag about his nephews like you do. I don't think a bad guy would stay loyal to his friends. And even though you've gotten into a little trouble, you've paid for your mistake. You don't even know it, but you've also been pretty lucky."

"Me?" Mark pointed back at himself. "Lucky?"

"Sure." Vic nodded. "I can think of a number of things you've told me that I would say were lucky."

"Name one."

"Okay, you remember telling me about your date with Linda? What was her last name?"

"McMurtry."

"Yeah, and how her old boyfriend chased you home and waited out in the street?"

"Yeah."

"And you came outside with a pistol?"

"Yeah."

"Well, you ever wonder what would've happened if he had gotten out of that car? What if, somehow that pistol went off? Things would be different for everyone—you, the old boyfriend, and even Linda herself. It could've easily happened, yet it didn't. Ever think about that?"

"I guess not."

"Well, think about it. That's just one little thing that could've turned out different. I'd say you were pretty lucky."

"I guess so." A few minutes passed before Mark continued, "What did you mean about being loyal to my friends?"

"The night you got in trouble. You never ratted on the guys that were with you?"

"No." Mark scratched his head. "I never did."

"I'm not saying that was right. I'm just saying you showed some loyalty for sticking it out alone."

"That's not exactly true." Mark stayed silent for a few seconds. He had grown to trust Vic, and he appreciated the things he was saying. He decided to put some cards on the table. "I didn't rat 'em out because I was such a great friend and being loyal. It was because I was scared of 'em. I was scared of what they'd do to me if they thought I squealed."

"Oh," Vic said. He took off his hat and rubbed at his scalp. "Well, I still say you're not such a bad guy." A serious expression came over his face. "By the way, I've been meaning to ask you something. Once we finish the community service, I was hoping you'd want to stay on as my coach."

"Really?"

"Really. It has to do with my own timeline. It's a goal of mine to play in a tournament. I was hoping maybe you'd be my coach."

"Really?"

"Really." Vic paused. "There's something else." Vic faced the sun. "I haven't been completely honest with you."

"What is it?" Mark felt a bond with Vic. "You going to tell me you can really see through them dark glasses?"

"That's pretty funny. But even I'm not that good of an actor."

"Just kidding."

"I know," Vic flashed a warm smile. "And what I have to tell you has to do with some kidding of my own. You see, all those stories I told you about the *stronzo* might not have been exactly as I told them."

"You made them up?"

"No, the stories were real. But, the *stronzo* wasn't some friend of mine. The truth is—the *stronzo* was me."

"Oh, man." Mark snorted. "That's your confession?"

"That's it. I told you all those stories because they were some of the lessons I learned the hard way. You should know that everyone does foolish things at some point—especially when you're young. The important thing is to learn from your mistakes and not repeat them. That's what growing up and becoming responsible is all about—not making the same stupid mistakes over and over."

Mark smiled and placed his hand on Vic's shoulder. "I would've never guessed you were the *strunze*."

"Like I said kid, we *all* are at one point or another. And I'll go one further. Here's something I've only told Angela."

Mark swallowed hard. "What's that?"

"Even though the insurance companies and lawyers all said it wasn't my fault, I still feel like I could've done something different to prevent what happened to me. I've spent many sleepless nights thinking about it. If only I had stood somewhere else. If, maybe all the safety equipment was on different. If only I could've known what was coming.

"But then I realized—it doesn't matter." Vic threw up his hands. "What's done is done. I'm the one that has to live with it. It took me a while, but I decided it wasn't worth losing sleep over. I couldn't go back in a time machine and do it over. Besides, I'd rather something like this happen to me than to Angela or anyone else close to me. In that sense, I think I'm lucky about the whole thing. You know what I mean?"

"Yeah, I think so." Mark felt a need to share something. "I got something of my own that I've never told anybody."

"What's that kid?"

"Ever since I was little—" Mark hesitated, and then continued. "I've kind of been afraid of the dark."

Vic nodded and rubbed his chin. "You know what they say?"

Mark shook his head.

"There ain't nothing in the dark that ain't there in the light."

On his way home from the golf course, Mark took a different route. He crept down the overgrown alley and peeked through a slat in the fence. When he didn't spot anything in the backyard, Mark started to doubt his suspicions.

Maybe it's too late.

He ducked through a gap near a hedge and looked toward the house. He grew nervous. 'I'm looking for Fluffy.' Mark devised as an excuse. 'Have you seen him?' It should appease Skeeter or Moose if they spotted him snooping around their backyard. 'He's missing again and there's a reward of five bucks if I can find him.' Fluffy was the cat that lived next door with an elderly couple.

Mark moved stealthily around a heap of worn tires and
hopped onto a pile of salvaged planks piled against the detached
garage. He rubbed dust from the back window and cupped his hands
around his eyes. Inside, he saw a paint-stained drop cloth covering a
vehicle. Most of it was hidden, but he could make out a rear quarter
panel. It was a Thunderbird. And even in the dim light, he could tell it
was cherry red. Mark knew the true owner. He once tried to wash the
same car.

Mark counted each concrete step as he climbed toward the station house entrance. At nine, he dropped a smoldering cigarette and squashed it with the twisting sole of his boot. At fourteen, he almost stepped into a gooey wad of chewing gum. He reached the top landing at twenty, and then took a deep breath.

Just keep going.

The effects of gravity were weighing heavy. Mark moved like a turtle with a biological burden loaded on his back. He had to summon a reserve of energy just to reach out and press the latch. He tugged the wooden door. Once inside, he looked beyond the front desk to the booking area. A scruffy-looking individual sat with his head lowered. The man, wobbling and slobbering, wasn't going anywhere; he was handcuffed to the bench.

Anxiety rose and Mark wanted to shrink inside a protective shell. He started to turn for the exit, but a sergeant at the front desk pinned him to the spot.

"What can I do for you?"

"I-I-I'd like to talk to Officer Bellamy." Mark's voice was a little shaky. It had been a few months since first meeting Officer Bellamy, but it felt like years. A change had occurred. It happened slowly, kind of like a dripping faucet.

"Bellamy, eh? Who should I say is asking?"

"Mark." He remembered that rainy afternoon on Granny's front porch and the officer's kind demeanor; it was enough to determine whom to approach. "My name's Mark Crowe."

"Right then." The desk sergeant lifted the receiver and dialed a few numbers. "Let's see if he's in." He kept his eyes focused on Mark. "Yeah, it's Archie at the front desk. Tell Bellamy there's some kid named Mark here to see 'em." He hung up the phone. "Have a seat." He pointed. "He'll be down soon."

Relieved to have gotten this far, Mark eased his backside into the cane webbing of a chair. A disinfecting pine scent lingered from an early morning mopping. He was flanked by flags standing in polished brass bases. A spotlight shone on the facing wall where photos of previous commanders hung alongside various achievement plaques. It wasn't his first time in the precinct house, but it was his first visit through the front door.

For days, Mark had mulled over his options. Initially, he thought about the timeline and to steer clear of Moose and Skeeter. If they wanted to commit a crime, he didn't want to be involved. If anyone asked any questions, he would play deaf, dumb, and blind. Fear of retaliation was enough of a motivating factor to keep him quiet in the golf cart disaster, and he would remain silent again. So what if they went ahead with the plan? Things would just have to resolve themselves on their own.

But an inner voice told him something different.

Maybe it was the sessions with Mr. Shannon. At first, Mark was leery of the process. He waffled and fudged his way through, confident in his knack for storytelling to give the right answers. As contentment settled in, he realized it wasn't an exam and he wasn't trying for a passing grade. It took some time, be he figured out that he wasn't there to impress Mr. Shannon. Mark discovered that he was there to acknowledge the bits and pieces of his own reality. As more of the truth leaked out, he began to accept it, and felt the sessions did some good. He even tipped off Mr. Shannon about the stolen car scheme before it occurred.

But the new voice didn't think that was enough.

Maybe Granny's trip to the hospital had changed him. The only real loss he ever felt was when Pappy died. Mark was nine years old at the time and didn't find out from his mother until weeks after it had occurred. He remembered feeling sad for a few days. Pappy was the only person he felt was on his side. But now, after years of living together, he felt an even stronger attachment to Granny. She gave him something he never had; a feeling of permanence. She provided a safe haven. Without her, there was no one else; his last hope. Before she went to the hospital, Mark had never thought of her possible demise. Loosing Granny would bring him real pain. Thoughts of her wellbeing flooded him with emotion; feelings he had never known before. Although it wasn't perfect, Granny's house was now his home, and he no longer took that stability for granted.

Realizing those emotions must have changed him in some way.

And then there was Vic. Whether it was the time or the stories they shared, a bond formed that Mark wanted to hold onto. Vic had become his mentor, his teacher, his guide; something he never had or knew was missing. Vic's sage advice seemed corny at times, but the principles from a positive role model had given Mark confidence and encouragement. Until Vic came along, no one had ever taken an interest in Mark. And now, they were partners of a sort. They relied and depended on each other. They shared a trust. Mark never felt that important about anything. He also learned that Vic could see better than anyone he knew. It would be days before he could consult with Vic, so he did the next best thing; he thought about what Vic's advice would be.

Mark then realized his own voice was telling him the same thing. *This whole thing's like the apple tree—sour and sweet.*

"I'm Bellamy," the officer said, pushing through a swinging gate in the banister. "Lucky you caught me. What can I do for you?"

Mark stood. "I don't know if you remember me or not, but you were at my house a while ago. I think you also helped setting up my community work with Vic Adano, you know, on the golf course."

"Yeah." Officer Bellamy cracked a smile. "I know who you are. You're Colonel Crowe's grandson. I hardly recognized you."

Mark took a deep breath. "I-I-I got something I'd like to talk to you about."

"Sure, what's on your mind?"

"It might take awhile." Mark looked around. "Is there a place we could sit down?"

"Sure, follow me."

Officer Bellamy held the gate open and Mark stepped through. It felt like plunging right into a tiger's den. They climbed a flight of stairs and emerged into a bustling open space. Pairs of desks with their fronts pushed together were aligned making it look like square islands in a sea of polished linoleum. Each desktop contained a similar telephone, lamp, and calendar. Nameplates, family photos, and varying heights of stacked files made them different.

An empty chair for visitors clung to the side of each desk. "Have a seat," Officer Bellamy said, pointing to an adjacent one. "You remember my partner?" He pointed across desktop clutter. "Officer Gagnon."

Mark hadn't noticed him as they approached. He turned slightly to see the same cop that previously rubbed him the wrong way. Mark tried to stay calm. "Hey," Mark said, offering a casual wave.

The partner appeared indifferent. He offered a nod, then picked up the telephone, tapped it to his ear, and ran a finger through an opened file.

Mark eased into the chair and rested an elbow on Officer Bellamy's desktop.

Officer Bellamy tilted back in his swivel chair. "Okay, what've you got for me?"

"I-I-I'm not sure exactly where to start." Mark reached over to grab a pen. He started spinning it on the desktop. "You see, I might know something about a certain crime." *Keep yourself out of this.* "Not that I have anything to do with what might have happened, you see. I had nothing to do with it." *Should've had a better plan.* "I just happened to know the people that might have something to do with it." *Man, this place is creepy.*

"Go ahead. I won't jam you up with anything if you're not involved."

Behind Mark, the phone receiver returned to its cradle with a clatter.

"Hey, now I remember you," the partner interrupted. "You're the one throwing golf balls at cars."

Mark sensed an axe falling on him. He mumbled, "Like I said before, that wasn't me." *This dude's definitely not part of the plan.*

"Well I didn't believe you then, and I don't believe you now," the partner looked across at Officer Bellamy. "I told you we should have run him in."

Officer Bellamy shook his head.

Mark lowered his head; it felt like it weighed a hundred pounds. He tried to conserve his energy. *Stay calm.* If only he had a protective shell to deflect and frustrate what felt like a predator's strikes.

Casters squeaked as Officer Gagnon pushed back from his desk. "Yeah, you told us all right." He nodded and let loose a mocking laugh. "But one thing's for sure, you're the one that tore up all those golf carts." He plopped his steel-toe shoes on the desktop. "You going to tell me that wasn't you?"

Stay calm. You're doing the right thing. Sour apples.

"Anyway," Officer Bellamy said. "What is this you might know something about?"

Mark turned to face Officer Bellamy and searched for the right words. "Over at the golf course, there're these rumors about someone's car being stolen."

"What kind of rumors?"

"Well, I'm not sure where he lives, see, but the rumor is one of the guys had his car stolen. That's where I heard about it—at the golf course."

"What's the guy's name?"

"Luke Dengel."

"Dengel?"

"Yeah, drives a Thunderbird. You know, one of them collectables."

Officer Bellamy gestured with a nod in his partner's direction, "You know anything about a stolen vehicle?" He looked down at his notes, "A Thunderbird belonging to someone named Dengel?"

"Check with Manero and Wilson. I think they caught a case like that," his partner said.

"I'll check." Officer Bellamy turned back to Mark. "What is it you want to tell us?"

Mark fidgeted with the pen, searching for the right words.

"So—" The partner smirked at Mark. "You've graduated to stealing cars now?"

Frustration began to boil. *Stay calm.* "No—" Mark growled through clenched teeth. "I'm here to help, man."

"Help?" He let out a sarcastic chuckle. "You got to be kidding? With your record, why should we believe you?"

"Because I'm telling you I had nothing to do with it."

"I think you've told us lies before."

That does it. Mark slammed his palm down on the desk. He stood and turned to face the partner. "Look man, I've paid for my mistakes. I came here trying to do some good, so get off my back!"

"Whoa, whoa," Officer Bellamy said. "Have a seat, he's just kidding around."

The partner said, "Wrecking golf carts?"

"C'mon man," Mark shot back. "That was a different time—I wasn't thinking too good. Besides, I did my time."

"You know, it's not a big leap from wrecking golf carts to stealing cars."

Mark glared. *Man, one of these days, man…*

Someone in dress shirt, tie, and gold badge yelled from a doorway, "The Captain wants everyone in the conference room A.S.A.P."

"Must be the Mayor on the horn," said Officer Bellamy.

"You wait here." The partner pointed at Mark. "We're not done with you."

Within seconds, the room fell silent.

Mark looked around and saw a few secretaries talking into their phones and a clerk delivering mail from a cart. He squirmed in the chair and drummed his fingers on the desktop.

I should just get out of here. The time was perfect for a clean getaway. Mark reached over to a notepad, scribbled down an address, tore it out, folded it, and left it in the center of Officer Bellamy's desk. He calmly stood and walked unnoticed out of the busy station house.

Mark felt lighter.

I got an interesting call from Officer Bellamy this week," Mr. Shannon said, rocking back in his swivel chair. "He said they received an anonymous tip that helped crack a stolen car case."

Mark was caught by surprise. "Anonymous?"

"He said it was anonymous, but the way he hinted to a few things, it sounded more like he had a good idea of where the tip came from."

Mark remained silent.

"He said they recovered the car without a scratch on it. The owner was ecstatic. They got it back to him in one day."

Mark wasn't sure if Mr. Shannon was on a fishing expedition looking for more hot tips, or if he was actually trying to congratulate him for a job well done. The same sense of uncertainty lingered around him for days.

Most of his time was spent holed up indoors. Mark didn't want to be seen anywhere near the McMurtry's house or the golf course. A feigned illness kept him from school. He burned up hours secure in the recliner watching television and imagining numerous scenes unfolding down the street.

Flashing lights. Bullet-proof vests. SWAT teams. Megaphone commands. Smoke bombs. Guns drawn. "Come out with your hands up!" Ramming doors. Skeeter and Moose handcuffed. "You have a right to remain silent." Paddy wagon ride. Body odor. Fingerprint inkpad. Flash bulbs. "Turn sideways." Shuffling chains. Latches clasping. "Put this on." Buzzing doors. Blank stares.

Mr. Shannon flashed a genuine smile in his direction. "You know, whoever gave them the tip did a real nice thing for the community."

"Officer Bellamy said that?"

"He said it. I say it too. He suggested I make a note in your file, because you did the right thing, and came to see him about something that turned out helpful."

Mark said, "Yeah?" He sat thinking for a few seconds. "You think it was enough for a free shopping spree?"

"Who knows?" Mr. Shannon smiled. "Doing a good thing is often its own reward. As for us, looks like you made it—this will be our last meeting."

Mark nodded. "That's cool."

"As I recall, you had ideas of running away. What was it you said, 'skipping town'?"

"Yeah, well, I still could."

"Well, I hope you don't. And I'm happy you made it."

"No big deal."

"If you'll allow me, I'll give you one last bit of advice. No matter how fast or how far you run, you can never leave your troubles behind. The only way to get rid of them is to stop running and deal with them head on."

"Man." Mark shook his head. "You're starting to sound like my sister."

"She's always giving good advice?"

"No, she's always nagging and preaching."

"Anyway, I hope you don't hold any grudges."

"Nope, just glad it's over."

"And your community service, I'm glad that's worked out."

"Yeah, it hasn't been all bad."

"After your first few times with Mr. Adano, I wasn't so sure."

"Why's that?"

"You may've not known, but I checked in regularly with Mr. Adano. Early on, he told me a few things that had me wondering if it was going to work out."

Mark couldn't explain why, but he felt hurt. "Why would he say that?"

"It wasn't anything he said. As a matter of fact, you're lucky Mr. Adano got involved. Most others would've lost patience with you and some of your antics."

"What'd he say?" Suddenly, knowing what Vic thought about him was the most important thing in the world.

"He said he liked you. You reminded him of himself when he was younger."

"Really. He said that?"

"Yeah. But your first few sessions didn't go all that well." Mr. Shannon leaned his elbows on the desktop. "He told me about times when he was talking or asking a question and it seemed you didn't answer, or had jumped from one side of him to another. A couple of times, he waited in one spot for long periods of time. When you caught up, you smelled like cigarette smoke. There were times he swore he thought you were deliberately pointing him in the wrong direction and giving him bad advice on where to hit the ball."

"C'mon man." Blood rushed from Mark's face. "He said that?"

"He said you may have skipped a few holes here and there too." Mr. Shannon leaned back and placed his hands behind his head. "But here's the thing—he never gave up on you. I told him he was under no obligation to continue. I tried to give him advice on how to handle each situation. I told him he could confront and challenge you anytime. I gave him every opportunity to walk away at anytime. Each time he would simply say that he'd like to handle it his own way."

"Look, I can't believe you're telling me all this." Mark didn't know what else to say. He sat in silence for a while. He wanted to get angry and return with a counter attack. Yet he knew Vic's suspicions were basically true.

I guess facing up to this is the right thing to do.

"Come to think of it," Mark said. "Maybe a few of those things did happen, but only when we first started. Things were different then."

"That's right, and that's the point." Mr. Shannon leaned forward. "And just for your information, I also know you played golf with Mr. Adano even when you were told not to." He interlocked his fingers, placed them behind his head, and then rocked back. "But all of that's in the past too. You see, things worked out."

He looked Mr. Shannon in the eye. "I'm glad Vic didn't give up."

"So am I."

"While we're on the subject of coming clean," Mark said. "I guess you figured out that some of the stories I've told you, well, I kind of stretched the truth."

There. He won't pull anymore surprises on me.

Mr. Shannon smiled. "I've been doing this a long time, Mark. But it's good of you to acknowledge your shortcomings."

"Yeah."

"We'll just leave it at that," Mr. Shannon smiled. "I am curious though. Why you would feel the need to make up stories?"

Mark thought for a few seconds. "I guess it's just something I always do. The only time people listen to me is when I have something interesting to say. So, I make up stories sometimes. If people like my stories, then maybe they'll like me."

"Interesting." Mr. Shannon rested his worn wingtips on the desktop. "You certainly have given me a lot to think about. I'll even give you credit for trying to work on a few things. Your descriptions of the 'perfect dad' took a lot of thought. Do you realize I never really asked about your father?"

"I never thought to talk about it."

"I figured you'd bring it up if you wanted to."

"I guess," Mark looked at the clock, "mainly, because I don't know much about him myself."

"This may be your last chance."

"I've been told so many different stories I don't know what to believe. They range from he's dead, to he ran off and left us, to he was abducted by aliens. Bottom line, I've never known the truth, man. Even if I wanted to find him, I wouldn't know where to look, or how to look, or even what to look for." Mark glanced at Mr. Shannon. "Not that I'm looking or anything."

"Maybe someday you'll be curious."

"Maybe. But I still think about the 'perfect dad' thing."

"You do?"

"Sure. You know, being around Vic so much, and listening to some of the stuff he tells me, gives me the idea that he would probably be a pretty good dad. I like being around Vic." Mark grinned. "He's cool. Even though he's more like a big brother, I'd probably put him on the list. If you asked me today who I think would be the 'perfect dad,' I'd definitely say, Vic."

Mark sat at the cleared kitchen table eating a second piece of cake. He watched as Granny washed the last of the dishes while his sister dried and returned each one to an open cabinet. "I think this is the best chocolate cake I ever tasted," he said.

Granny turned to him and said, "I'm so glad you think so dear." Dishwater stained the front of her apron a darker shade.

"You should like it," his sister said, her back to him. "It was your choice."

With a wrinkled hand, Granny wiped the counter then pulled the sink stopper. Used water gurgled down the drain. Hunched over, she shuffled towards Mark and settled into a chair. She took a deep breath. "I guess the next time we have a party, it will be for graduation."

"Yeah," Mark said, licking his fork. "I guess so." He stood and handed the dish to his sister. "Here's one more."

She raised her eyebrows.

"I knew I could make it," Mark said, returning to the seat next to Granny.

"I knew it too," she said, patting his hand. "So, tell me, how were Pappy's clubs today?"

"They did real good."

"Did you make a birdie?"

"Not today Granny." Mark looked toward the ceiling. "I wasn't that good."

"But you always make a birdie."

"I guess not today."

"Oh well," Granny gushed. "Pappy would still be proud."

Mark's sister joined them at the table. "I hope the boys didn't embarrass you too much with all their questions about the guide dog."

"Embarrass me?" Mark stuck one of his thumbs to his chest. "No way. I only wish Vic would have brought Buck along."

"With all the confusion here, he was probably smart to leave him home." Mark's sister rested her elbows on the table. "By the way," she said, "you must be feeling like a king today."

"A king?"

"Yeah, having everybody sing to you, having your favorite food served to you, playing golf with your friend and having them over for dinner. And—" She stuck a finger in the air. "Blowing out eighteen candles."

"Actually, if you want to know the truth, my favorite food is scrambled eggs, but I knew we couldn't have breakfast for dinner." Mark smiled. "Besides that, I guess you're right."

"There's not enough room on any cake to hold all my candles," Granny said, "I'd need the fire department to help me put them out." She smiled. "I sure like Vic. And that Angela is just an angel. I can tell she really loves that man."

Mark nodded.

Mark's sister moved her hands wildly. "I just love his accent and how he talks so much with his hands. And it's so cute how he calls you *Marco* and his *pie-zahn-oh*. What's a *pie-zahn-oh*?"

"I'm not sure." Mark grinned. "But I think it's something good."

Granny said, "And I like your new haircut."

Mark reached to where the long locks use to hang and found nothing there.

"And you look so handsome in that shirt."

"Don't get used to it all. I'm just trying something different."

"Well," Granny turned misty-eyed, "you look nice."

Mark's sister craned her neck and raised her voice. "Hey Tom."

"Yeah." A grouchy voice traveled from the living room.

"What're doing in there?"

"I'm trying to watch the ballgame."

"The boys with you?"

"No, but I can hear 'em on the front porch."

Mark's sister rolled her eyes then turned back to Mark. "So, Mister Eighteen, Mister Adult, Mister No More Worries, what are you going to do now?"

"I told you I could make it."

"We're all so proud," Granny said.

"Well—" Mark put on his serious face. "It's like this. You see, Vic asked me the same thing. He said your whole life is kind of like that. You know, a bunch of little timelines you string together. He said it was important to think about what was next. So, I've been thinking about it and I've come up with something."

"What is it?"

"Making sure I graduate."

"That's not too far off."

"I counted on the calendar—only ten weeks."

"What about your attendance, and your grades?"

"Oh, there may be a few things I need to work on, but I think I got enough time to straighten 'em out."

"How wonderful," murmured Granny.

"You probably think I've been a little harsh with you," his sister said. "But it was only to get your attention." She hesitated. "If you need help, let me know."

"Thanks, but I think I can make it. And I've already been thinking about the next timeline after that."

"After graduation?"

"I figured I would need some kind of job. You see, that was another thing Vic told me about, between the apple trees, bird calls, and turkey potpies."

Mark's sister looked confused. "Apple trees and turkey potpie?"

"Yeah, it's a long story. But basically, he kinda told me that just staying out of trouble isn't enough. It's really not that big a deal. It's what everybody should be doing automatically. Anyway, he gave me the idea about being an adult."

His sister just nodded.

Mark continued. "It means you have to take responsibility for things you do."

Her eyes grew bigger.

"It's got me thinking," Mark said, rubbing his chin. "I know I cost you some money with all the lawyers and stuff. Well, I want you to figure out how much all of that was, and I want to pay you some of it back."

Mark's sister's mouth fell open.

"Pappy would be so proud," Granny said.

Terry Corvid opened the front door and yelled in the house, "Hey Mark, come outside."

Granny and his sister stared at each other with misty eyes and smiles on their faces as Mark rose from the table.

"Let me see what they want," he said and plotted a course through the living room.

A cheer from the crowd erupted from the television followed by analysis from the color commentator. Tom was huddled on the edge of the sofa and leaned toward the screen with his eyes glued to the gridiron. He pumped a fist when the official signaled for a first down.

Mark pulled the front door knob and stepped over the threshold. He stood on a crack in the concrete porch and watched two pairs of swaying legs, too short to reach the ground, goading the porch swing like it was an amusement park ride. Links in the chain moaned and popped. He leaned over to right an overturned pot of marigolds, and then kicked some of the spilled soil from the overhang.

Corey was gripping the armrest with one hand and trying to twist the taut chain links with the other. The front of his shirt was covered with a new coat of dirt to match the smear of chocolate icing. "We want to hear a story," he said.

"Yeah, make it a good one," Terry said, kicking his feet in the air to make his untied shoelaces flutter.

"Let me think about one." Mark tossed his head, but the strands of hair he expected to follow were no longer there. The new haircut took some time to get used to. "Move over and make room."

Mark perched between the boys. The wooden swing creaked. His legs reached the ground and regulated the sway. "Well you see, when I was your age I use to have a friend that wasn't too smart," Mark thought for a second and smiled. He gestured with a hand. "I called him *strunze*."

The two boys looked at each other.

One of them said, "What's a *strunzel*?"

CPSIA information can be obtained at www.ICGtesting.com
Printed in the USA
LVOW101308230212

270070LV00004B/3/P